CHOCOLATE DOVE :
A TWISTED LOVE STORY

by

Patrick Jackson

DORRANCE
PUBLISHING CO
EST. 1920
PITTSBURGH · PENNSYLVANIA 15222

Dorrance Publishing Co
585 Alpha Drive
Pittsburgh, PA 15238
Visit our website at www.dorrancebookstore.com

ISBN: 979-8-89341-101-0

eISBN: 979-8-89341-600-8

LETTER THE FROM AUTHOR

THIS COMPILATION BOOK IS COMPRISED OF TWO BOOKS. THE FIRST OF WHICH IS ORIGINS LILITH'S REVENGE AND THE SECOND TITLED IMPOSTOR. ING A TWISTED LOVE STORY IS THE FIRST ARC IN THE CHOCOLATE DOVE SERIES. THE NEXT ARC WILL CONTINUE THE STORY IN DECEITFUL DEATH ARC. DECEITFUL DEATH WILL CONSIST OF UNHOLY UNION (BOOK 3) AND DEATH OF SORROW (BOOK 4). HOPE YOU ENJOY THE STORY AND THE TWISTS.

The Eyes of me follow and you'll see that together as we walk along this journey follow the eyes of the story

A TWISTED LOVE STORY Arc

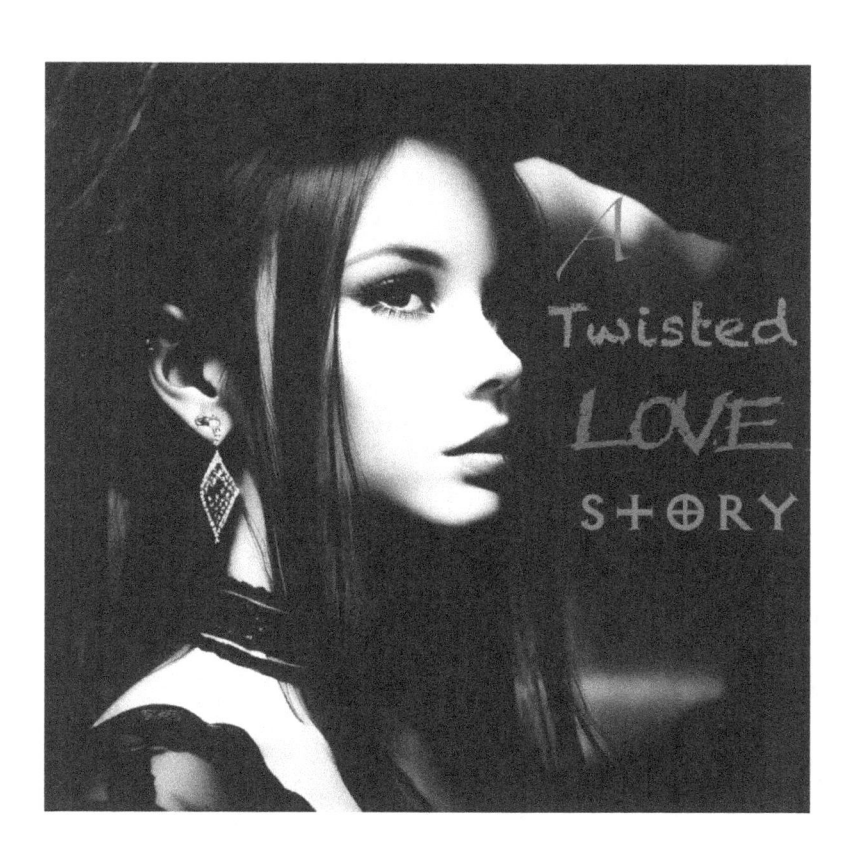

A
Twisted
LOVE
STORY

Origins

Lilith's

Revenge

THE CHOCOLATE DOVE ORIGINS : LILITH'S REVENGE

The beauty of a dove is vibrant and bright, even more so at night. Giving birth to a Chocolate Dove, which happens to be a visual delight, especially during its flight. The Chocolate Dove has many lanes with few gains. It travels searching for peace, but leaves destruction in its wake. To take the Chocolate Dove into your home is the equivalent of losing your heart in a dice game. Risky but so is love, but the Chocolate Dove is above love, it only knows the doves and doves don't love. They fly and leave people stunned, never asking why anyone would ever love a dove. Without it being gunned first, leading to bloodthirst. The Chocolate Dove is self-perverse to do its worst to anyone who seems like a threat. The Chocolate Dove gives no reason to fret, at least not yet. As time passes, the Chocolate Dove seems to like you more than usual, it can't comprehend the feeling. It's intense, becoming increasingly difficult to revolt its interesting pressure. The Chocolate Dove immerses itself into you only to fly away out of fear, so it hurts you time after time until you let it go. The Chocolate Dove comes back to find that you have left with nothing behind. The Chocolate Dove is perplexed and attempts to flex its wings to soar high, but it's too much. The Chocolate Dove is faced with a burden for the uncertain is unclear time is a sorrow's Lear a king without a kingdom ignorance's freedom and love's fool alone without its heart as the tool opposed to appearing cool by being cold, the Chocolate Dove realizes the mistake of flying free. It's empty and shallow, a mirrored hallow disgraced by the place. The chocolate dove turns back to find the one it left, the one that wishes it stayed, and now the chocolate dove has strayed so far but not far enough. Searching for the one it left behind. Finding the one sought after is within reach but cannot be breached. For the one the chocolate dove is after doesn't want to be scorned again, so the chocolate dove believes this is the end, but little does it know the one it wants. Wants it but cannot have it hoping the chocolate dove can understand that this isn't the end it's until we meet again my friend. The chocolate dove becomes mournful, reminiscent of the times it was loved unconditionally. Filled with shame and rage, the chocolate dove flies to search for what it has squandered away. Thinking to itself, "How could I've been so careless and complacent!?!" I had a love unyielding and true. I was loved beauty and flaws. I was loved with it all. Realizing the horrendously heavy weight of this fact, the chocolate dove spiraled into a graceless fall of depression and guilt as if it were a witness to its own happiness being murdered before its very eyes. The chocolate dove drags its bleeding heart, irate that its consequences were misled by its actions. Reasoning with itself downplaying its errors. Saying to itself it isn't my fault they just don't know how to love me. I'm perfectly built. Then the chocolate dove hears a beautiful and sweet angelic child. The child states that the chocolate dove is a beautiful creature, one that they hadn't had the pleasure or luxury of seeing a majestic beauty let alone hear one.

The chocolate dove is taken aback. Gasps, "Woody Woodpecker, pecking my front door. You can pecking understand me!?"

"Yes," the child says. "Let me explain."

"You go right ahead, weirdo."

"Hey, that's not nice."

"What? You're the one who can talk to animals. Wait, you can talk to other animals, right?"

"Well, if you would let me explain, you rude little turd bird."

"Hey, hurtful."

"Just stating facts."

"Yeah, but turd bird? Really kid?"

"Yes, because you have a crappy attitude and my name isn't "kid," it's Re'nae."

"What kind of name is Re'nae?"

"A nice one. what's yours tur..."

"Don't you finish that, it's chocolate dove because I remind people of ebony chocolate."

"What's ebony chocolate?"

"You'll know when your older, Re'nae. It goes along with orientation."

"What's orientation?"

"For mature audiences, not kids."

"But for turd birds."

"Yes, for turd... I hate you."

"For why?"

"For I don't know. Back to explaining."

"Oh alright. Well, you see, I can only hear sadness. Once an animal finds joy, I can't hear them."

"What if an animal is sad because it can't talk to you again?"

"I'm not sure. It hasn't happened to me yet. I could hear you falling and I wanted to catch you."

"Well, thanks for the save."

"I was curious about what was plaguing you."

"Plaguing me? Are you saying I'm sick or something?"

"No, I was merely asking what's troubling you."

"Troubling me? Ain't nothing troubling me. I'm a baddie with a fatty.

I'm beautiful, hot, and cool. Why would I be troubled?"

"That was clearly a display of grandstanding with attempts to elude me that you're perfectly content but I hate to disillude you."

"Re'nae, how old are you? What's with the college words? Aren't you a kid?"

"Blame my father, he always used big words to explain small situations. But his practice and constant strive to broaden my vocabulary is what has become of me here before you."

"O..K.. then... get to your little analysis of me. See what I did there? I can use big words too. But I'll break it down for you too. Analysis is someone asking their sister, "Why anal?"

"You know don't have to be a smart ass, turdbird."

"Well, get on with it."

"Are you ready to hear this?"

"Get to it!"

"You're running."

"Running?"

"Yes, running from your issues, and those issues are you mistreated someone and took them for granted."

4

"Well, that's a little presumptuous of you."

"Let me be frank then. You're in love and you messed it up. But you don't want to own up to your actions, so you're placing it on any and everything but yourself. You believe you can change the narrative and for this reason I can hear you. Talk to you. Understand you."

"Why would you do that for me?"

"Even a chocolate dove deserves love."

"Love? What is love?"

"Oh baby, don't hurt me. Don't hurt me. No more. That's the one and a good song too."

"No, you're mistaken. I'm not in love with anyone but I'm in search of the keeper that set me free."

"Oh, really? What were they like?"

"My keeper? Oh, they were wonderful. I was treated with respect and compassion. Given shelter and food. Warmth and fuzzy feelings. You know, all that jazz."

"Sounds like they loved you."

"Yeah, but I don't see how they could do such a thing though."

"Why do you say that?"

"Looking back, I was a major turd bird."

"Hey, don't be so hard on yourself."

"I deserve this pain. I had everything."

"Yes, and you made a mistake."

"A huge one."

"Well, what are you gonna do about it?"

"I'm actually on a quest to find myself and my keeper so far it's been half assed. But I know i have to make amends and make this right for both of us. Thank you, Re'nae, for straightening me out... Huh!?! Where did you go?"

As the chocolate dove found its resolve, the child disappeared without a word or warning. Upon disappearing the ambiance began to slowly change. Revealing a stoic gothic site.

As the chocolate dove slowly ventured forward and a beautiful black granite shrine came into view. A gorgeous replica of Re'nae stands towering over the chocolate dove as it inspects further. Reaching the base of the grave in between two black waterfalls lies the grave of Re'nae. The epitaph inscribed on the cradle reads. "Here lies the daughter of Ophelia, our queen of magic and profit of peace. Re'nae was blessed with the ability to hear sorrows and give guidance despite her small stature. She was bestowed great wisdom beyond her years from her mother and incredible bravery from her father. Which led to her untimely demise. She was renowned for her kindness and became known as sorrow's ear and the siren of the voiceless. She gave her life for her people selflessly. She will be forever guiding weary souls to peace protecting them on their journey."

"So Re'nae is dead!?"

"Yes, she is."

"Who tf said that!?!"

"'Twas I, the guardian of this crypt, tasked with protecting the remains of my king and Queen Ophelia's beloved princess Re'nae. Now speak and show yourself trespasser!"

"Uh dude down here. Why can you understand me? Also FYI, I was just talking to Re'nae before all this appeared."

"What?!? How could this be?"

"How could that be? She caught me out of the air when I was falling from the sky."

"You caused the princess to awaken? Astonishing! What could have caused this, I wonder?"

"Well, I was struggling with my keeper setting me free. I left but I had every intention of coming back. But Re'nae helped me to see that I hurt my keeper. I damaged their heart. Now I must reprimand my foul actions and repair my transgressions."

"Such elegance and articulation. How are you capable of making it this far? Most would perish before ever setting foot at the entrance. Let alone make it to the princess's inner chamber."

"What's the big deal with this place anyway?"

"How dare you speak ill of this sacred memorial."

"I mean no disrespect. I simply have no rational idea why I'm here but believe me I have plenty of thoughts. Like am I dead? You'll tell me the truth, right Martin?"

"What did you say? Did you say Martin?"

"I did but I don't know why I said it. What does the name Martin mean to you crypt guardian?"

"It is my name and in the midst of this conversing, not once have I uttered any declaration of my birth title to you. So enlighten me on how you know concealed information like my identity."

"I don't know; it was like a memory."

"A memory?"

"Yes, a memory, Martin. So whilst I have your attention, you mind giving me some context on what happened to Re'nae?"

"That's Princess Re'nae ,show some deference."

"Deference?"

"RESPECT, you insolent winged dung."

"What's with you and Re'nae calling me a shit bird? The disrespect you royals have"

"It is because we're held to a higher standard; anything less is equivalent to horse feces."

"So why can't you guys say shit?"

"That is a curse word used to damn the condemned and punish the wicked."

"So you guys are righteous."

"Yes."

"Outta sight I dig it."

"Don't mock the royal family's decisions."

"I'm sorry, it just feels off."

"Doesn't matter how you feel, it's what's good for the people that the family protects."

"Ok, the protection aspects you keep preaching about and what the princess was berating me about. I get it peace, prosperity, and protection. Can someone just tell me why I'm here and what does this have to do with me?"

"I know not what includes you. Nevertheless, you are here, so I shall tell the tale of the princess... "Long ago Princess Re'nae was a fierce but compassionate warrior. That loved everything friend or foe alike she saw good in everyone's heart. The princess took on the problems of her kingdom's people. Her people's problems were her problems. The princess did things her way despite her parents' wishes. They knew she was brave but emotionally gullible. One fateful day she met another little girl that had no family. The princess took her in and the family accepted her as a part of the royal family. The little girl became the princess's little sister and most trusted best friend. The king named the little girl Lily. Declaring your name henceforth shall be Lily for the acronym: Lucky. I. Love. You. She grew into a beautiful royal maiden and a royal princess in her own right. But as time went on she began to wander the lands. Unaware of the dangers the royal lands held. Lily met a young boy all alone. Feeling the sadness she felt having been in this position earlier in her life took sympathetic empathy upon the young man. Remembering her sister's kind heart puts her hand out in acceptance. The young boy took her hand and grew quite fondly of the beautiful girl. He gazed into Lily's eyes wondering how a beautiful girl could exist. The infectious infatuation wasn't as innocent as it seemed for, you see, the young boy was conflicted. He was tasked with the mission of infiltrating the kingdom and destroying it from within. Looking into Lily's eyes his thoughts race and his heart beats faster. Thinking to himself what if I just live in the kingdom and never return here? Princess Lily brought word of the boy to her sister.

"Sister I've found a friend."

"Oh? From?"

"The outlands."

"Oh!!? Oh!! No! No! No! Take it back."

"He's not a dog."

"You don't know that!"

"He's like me. Alone without a family."

"Again you don't know that sister. When I found you, my heart was in it. When you found him, I believe heat was betwixt your legs in this decision."

"Re'nae, it's not all about if I like him. It's about having compassion like you did for me."

"So do you want him to be our brother?"

"No, but I don't want him to be alone out there."

"Lily I understand you like him but I feel something off about this."

"Please talk to mother and father."

"I make no promises, only acknowledgements. I have heard what you had to say. Don't make a fool of me. I'm going against my better judgment. You better be lucky I love you Lily."

"Really my whole name like that?"

"Straight like that, sis. This is a big ask. You won't be facing father, I will!"

"But you'll have Mother's..."

"Mother's what?"

"Hi Mom. Nothing, Lily's just babbling. We must be going now. Come on, sister."

"Alright, you girls have fun."

"We will. We'll talk about this later in-depth."

After speaking with her sister, Lily made her way back to the outlands where she came across the young boy once again.

"I have returned after having spoken with my sister about you. She has considered my request for her to endure an audience with our father endorsing you. Oh I'm sorry, where are my manners?!? I haven't introduced myself. I am Princess Lily of the royal lands and you are?"

"I am Lucian."

"What does Lucian mean?"

"I don't follow?"

"My father named me Lily as an acronym. Each letter represents a word that can be applied in a sentence. My name means "lucky I love you" but condensed it's Lily."

"I'm not sure I could think of anything meaningful about my name."

"Let me try. It's L-u-c-i-a-n, correct?"

"Yes."

"Alright how about Loyalty unwavering courageous individuals are noble."

"Wow that's a lot to live up to."

"Well then we just have to live it together and besides I believe in you."

"You don't even know me but the kindness you've shown me is astronomical. I will try to live up to the new name you have given me thankyou princess."

"You can call me Lily. I mean I would like it if you call me Lily."

"Sure thing Lily."

"Where is this going, Martin?"

"Your Lily's daughter and my niece."

"Princess? But how?"

"It took a while to figure it out but there was a reason I caught you. As well as to why you were summoned here. I promised your mother I would protect her and when I failed her I promised to protect her offspring."

"So you're my aunt, Re'nae?"

"Yes, but I had to be sure. Although granted that I rose from my grave to catch you, it's been decades since your parents died."

"Alright, so who's my father?"

"Weren't you listening to Martin?"

"The young boy that Lily wanted to save from the outlands is your father and the reason why me, your mom, and he himself are dead."

"My father is the reason that you're dead?"

"Yes, sadly me and your mom were betrayed by your father."

"He was in league with the black magic and death magic users. He taught your mother this curse that's placed upon me this very instant. I can't truly die because I am confined to this tomb to guide and train you."

"Train me for what?"

"To train you to properly use your powers."

"Powers? What powers!?"

"You were a human years ago when mother and father had you. What happened since then?:

"I've always been a bird, not a person. At least not while awake. At night I dream about the family I never had. I see how happy they were."

"Those weren't dreams, those were memories. You have the ability to realm switch. You can also shapeshift."

"How do I do that?"

"Well, you felt so trapped with my mother and father that you chose a bird and flew away. They thought you were kidnapped."

"So I'm a runaway?"

"For the most part yes, but you were enchanted by a sorrowfeeder."

"A sorrowfeeder?"

"A sorrowfeeder looks and sounds like a regular human. The key differences they have are that they're heartless for one and for two they feed off emotional pain. They continue discussing difficult issues that hurt you and insult you while pretending to be a friend. They don't stop until you either go insane or die. This realm calls them therapists."

"So that's why people that go to therapy come back suicidal."

"Yes but focus now on your true self."

"My true self?"

"Close your eyes and envision your human form. Concentrate, search your dreams and memories. Feel your true self find her across these converging realities. Find your inner Lucy."

"Inner Lucy?"

"Yes, your birth name is Lucy."

"Like the daughter of the devil?"

"Not quite but you do have dark powers now focus. What do you see?"

The chocolate dove scourer's her dreams and memories when she comes across a mirror with a door in it. I see a mirror with a door in it as I move closer the door opens with each step a woman begins to emerge. As I continue to approach, she begins coming closer.

"Who are you?" I ask.

"The woman says I am your subconscious and your human form. Step into the mirror, become me, and exit through the door."

Without a second thought, the chocolate dove stepped into the mirror becoming her true self. Exiting the door of her mind opening her eyes to see a beautiful chocolate complexion with smooth soft skin. After seeing her hands for the first time Martin conjures a full-body mirror.

The chocolate dove now reborn as Lucy, examines her body in private. She sees a beautiful curvaceous woman with long silky black hair with a height of 5ft 9in with green eyes. After viewing her body Lucy asks for clothes. Martin gives her a green top and black pants with white shoes that have black trim. Admiring herself in the mirror that Martin provided for her.

"Damn, I always knew I was a bitch but I never expected to be a bad bitch... Who am I kidding? Yes, I did, but still I'm so damn sexy."

"I'm elated that you've found your true self. I trust that in finding yourself you've also found your name as well?"

"Yes, the knowledge was instilled in me upon stepping into the mirror and obtaining my human body. My true identity and my birth name is Lucy."

"Yes, you are Lucy."

"Is there an acronym to my name as well?"

"Yes it stands for L.ove U.nited C.reated Y.ou. Their union as vile as it was to me created you and my sister lives in you so does the evil that got her killed."

"Ok, you're dead, right?"

"Yes, we established that and where are you going with this? Why couldn't she be enchanted or cursed like you?"

"Because a sorrowfeeder devoured her soul after giving birth to you. It tried to devour yours as well but your innocence and inability to comprehend pain and loss caused the sorrowfeeder to die. Sorrowfeeders can't survive without harvesting strife and sadness from living things."

"How did my father survive?"

"He fed on our enemies and criminals sentenced to death. As much as I wanted to save my people, murders, pedophiles, and war criminals were devoured by your father."

"He worked for the kingdom? Then what happened to garner so much hatred towards him?"

"He was tasked to bring down the kingdom from within. Your father betrayed me because of his brother's orders."

"His brother?"

"Yes, his brother and your uncle. Trenton is terrible to you..."

"Ha ha ha I bet he is."

"Excuse me?"

"Acronym, Re'nae you really didn't see what you said? T-i-t-t-y."

"Oh how funny Lucy but seriously, you should avoid your uncle until

22

you're ready to defeat him. It is because of his hand that I am here. By killing me he killed your mother. The betrayal and two lives at once ended up being more than she could handle."

"Why didn't my father let you die like my mother?"

"He bonded my soul to this chamber before I passed over for two reasons. One to atone for his betrayal and two to teach me his powers to train you if you should ever find your way here. He must have enchanted me to return here if I ever alerted Trenton."

"If so, smart move, good for that bastard for doing something decent. Alright moving on with my training. How long will it take?"

"About ten years."

"Ten years?!?!?! I know you f***ing lying."

"There is no need for foul magic words. It takes ten years to properly train outside of this chamber but time works differently here and our home realm. A day here is equivalent to two years outside in the realm your keeper comes from. This is the same for our realm. You have noticed that I've said realm and not country or state. This is because we reside amongst gods, myths, and the supernatural. We possess godlike beauty, knowledge, and strength. Judging your time out there you little freak."

"Why do I gotta be a freak?"

"Because I know what you're thinking, you nasty. I'll say this once but it really goes without saying but we also have peak sexual prowess."

"Oh hehe ain't nothing wrong with a little freaknasty from time to time ah."

"You're not in the streets anymore."

"The streets are in me for real for real. Wait, how do you know my slang?"

"A gentleman never asks and a lady never tells."

"Lucy, why won't you let me be great? Did you read my mind again?"

"That one, go with that. Let me find out you were in them streets with your royal ass."

"Bitch and what if I was?"

"I'm your senior you my junior don't twist the two again before your first lesson ends up being hand catching because you can catch them with that pretty new face you got."

"Damn bitch 0 to 100 real quick, why are you so hostile?"

"I'm sorry the inner thot in me wanted to drag a hoe but I'm classier now. But on my mama you bring that out again we're squaring up."

"Naw we don't need to do that. I got respect for the deceased. No disrespect in saying that. I'm just not trying to join you so soon. I'm gonna get off ghetto mode before I make changes to our bloodline."

"Better now?"

"Yeah thanks for that."

"You seemed kinda backed up."

"I've been here for two decades, that's fourteen thousand six hundred earth days."

"You were well overdue for a b-f."

"A b-f?"

"A bitch fit, we have them during the three h's."

"What's the three h's?"

"hangry, horny, hungry."

"Aren't hangry and hungry the same thing?"

"Hell no hangry is when you need a snack. Hungry is feed me and it better be what I like. Guys take notes or you bff could be bitch fit forever and us girls love forever and a day. Do you need a snack?"

"Yes, that would be lovely."

"How about cookies?"

"I haven't had a cookie in ages."

"Hey Martin, can you conjure up a batch of cookies for us?"

"Right away your highness."

"I'm not high yet Martin but until then there's no reason to be so formal."

"But your royalty madam."

"That may be true but I've lived my life as a pet bird in a cage until now, so you can just call me Lucy."

"Very well Madam Lucy."

"Close enough look cookies , thanks."

"Training first then finding your keepers agreed?"

"Agreed, let's get to it."

Elsewhere a menacing voice can be heard echoing down a long dark corridor. "How's it hanging, little brother? Looks like that daughter of yours finally embraced her roots or at least half of them anyway. I can't wait to meet her."

"Never, she doesn't even know about us."

"Oh is that right? So who turned her into a dove and caged her?"

"What?"

"You remember that girl you betrayed us for? You know the one that was head over heels for you."

"You don't mean!?"

"Hello Lucian, you look like you've seen a ghost."

"Lily !?! But how?? I watched you die."

"Yes you did and lord Trenton watched me rise from the dead."

"You resurrected her?!?"

"She's nothing but a husk of former self."

"Oh I do have my memories, Lucian, like how you betrayed me."

"I didn't betray you."

"You went insane, how can you serve Trenton? Lucy is your daughter as much as she's mine."

"You sure about that because the illusionary magic you call vision locking doesn't work on dead souls."

"So as I passed on I didn't see my dear sweet sister there."

"Did she really die?"

"No right?"

"My sister gave birth to Lucy not me so how dare you act like I'm an imbecile!"

"I loved you idiot and you go off and impregnate my sister??"

"I loved you Lily but you're delusional we had a relationship yes. But it wasn't intimate."

"You destroyed your home for a love that was one sided."

"The love you feel for me I feel for your sister."

"So you kill me?"

"She was carrying my child. You wanted to kill her, what was I supposed to do?"

"Let her die and be with me."

"You're sick Lily."

"You know what I'm tired of that name so since I was reborn I think a new name is in order."

"Remember the name I gave you?"

"You mean your sister gave me."

"Whatever anyways my new name shall be Lilith standing for L.ust I.s L.iving I.n T.his H.ell. Fitting, don't you think? Seeing that I was reborn from hell fire."

"Why are you putting Lucy in this?"

"Dumb question, you don't care. I don't and what better way to hurt everyone who hurt me by killing my darling niece. I had her caged in her bird form for the last twenty years. But since she's out searching for this fool it'll be a matter of time."

"What are you talking about?"

"The guy next to you, yeah, your daughter has a thing for him. He took care of her all these years and never knew. Kids?"

"Really Lilith, what have they done to you?"

"Absolutely nothing but maybe this will help you understand. You know the story of Adam and Eve, right?"

"Yeah, what of it? Eve wasn't the first woman she was the one that got pregnant and Lilith was shunned because of her desire to be on top. It's supposedly unholy to procreate in ways other than missionary. So Lilith became a demon and fed on the anguish of the parents as they endured the gruesome sight of their decimated child laying lifeless. Lilith was the first of the sorrowfeeders and our queen. The mother that was not to be and like my predecessor of my namesake before me I shall continue her work f**k them kids. Isn't she delightful?"

"Wow you sure do know how to pick'em Lucian. A woman after my own heart. I knew she was more than a nice piece."

"Thank you my lord, it seems I've chosen the wrong brother. Shall we make up for lost time and retire to your bed chamber?"

"That sounds like a swell idea, it's swelling already hehe. You stay here and listen to how a real man pleases a woman. Play with your pencil dick or something other than crying like a bitch."

"Hey Lilith, Re'nae was better, you basic bitch."

Lilith walks up to Lucian, grabbing him by his shirt, and pulling him into a kiss that would rival even the best of lovers. Finishing the kiss by locking eyes with Lucian as she feels and clutches his crotch.

She leans forward and whispers in his ear "It's really nice that you're trying to get me wet but I don't need your help. Your brother's voice does it for me and if I'm so basic, why are you so hard?"

Without warning, she pulls his shirt, slamming his face into the cage bars.

"Damn, that was hot baby bro."

"Come on you little voyeur. I need you to be the man that your little boy of a brother claimed to be. Mama needs to be punished."

"You heard her, I gotta go."

As Lilith and Trenton leave the other prisoner begins to speak. "Hey Lucian is it? What's going on? Why are we here? "

"You're the bait and I'm the surprise either way we're here to hurt Lucy."

"Who's Lucy? Lucy is my daughter and your dove that flew away."

"Wait, your daughter is a bird? You must be high on something."

"Without warning lucian transformed into a big black bear."

"Oh what the shit!?!"

"Forget what you know kid."

"You're a talking bear, I must be high. Hey do the thing."

"What thing?"

"The thing. The 'Only you can prevent...' thing."

"Oh ok only you can prevent dumbasses from being born. Wear a condom."

"That wasn't funny."

"Yeah and sitting in a cage is? Lucian says as he turns back to normal."

"Hey how do you still have clothes on when you transform?"

"I have a charmed necklace that allows safe storage when I pass through the mirror in my animal kingdom realm."

"Animal kingdom realm?"

"New guy forgot I'll explain in a second. Look kid this is not earth. So let's start off right, you know my name is Lucian, so what's yours?"

"My what?"

"Your name kid, everyone has one. what do people call you?"

"People call me orphan."

"Wait so you don't have a family?"

"No sir, I lived on the streets as a kid until Miss Lily took me in."

"Lilith you mean, when a woman makes an evil declaration it's best to address her in her title correctly."

"Yes well miss Lilith took me in when I was about 6 years old. She had a glorious house and a beautiful bird. I loved that bird but it flew away and never came back. I was heartbroken so I was in the process of moving for a better life. I left Miss Lilith a note. I expressed how I was grateful for the lessons and the shelter. I went on to say thankyou for the time with the bird until we meet again."

"Is that really what you said? I bet you wrote some poetic stuff. Elegance will get You caught up boy. But back to the point, your name?"

"I've always liked the names Nathan, Jamal, and Connor."

"So your name is Nathan Jamal Connors?"

"I like it."

"Good keep it moving now that we got your name figured out, let 's figure our situation out."

"What is our situation exactly? I mean what is this place? One minute I'm preparing a journey to find my life's path and then next I'm here."

"Well Nathan... scratch that I'm gonna call you Jamal. Calling you Nathan just feels like you're destined to do something very goddamn stupid. So understand that my daughter is infatuated with you. Doing something stupid isn't a luxury that you can't afford and a burden I don't wanna carry. Now Jamal this is the long and the short of it. You are in a realm where the supernatural, gods, and demons all converge. This is a hell,paradise, and paradox. You die here, your soul is taken for a sorrowfeeder's dinner. This place we're in is their kingdom. We are prisoners. You for baiting my daughter and me for emotional damage."

"Damn Lilith is truly twisted, spilling all your tea like that. I could actually use a twisted tea right about now."

"Jamal, your Nathan is showing. Turn down the stupid alright focus now."

"How many times are you gonna tell me that?"

"Uh until you do it. Look around and think. She nullified my powers with that kiss. Maybe if she did that a lil lower and more often Lucy would be her daughter."

"What was it?"

"I could've sworn I heard a limp dick say my magnificent name. Interrupting a great physical rodeo. Let's just say if I was a cowgirl I would've just won four hundred fifty rodeo buckles for the eight second ride. You do the math, nerds."

"That's discipline your ex has whew."

"What can I say I'm the bitch that keeps on giving. I hope you idiots don't try to escape the enchanted cells again because they will kill unruly prisoners. They will kill you and transmute your corpses into bars."

"The bars are corpses?!?"

"Yep, don't worry you'll be a part of the cells soon, just be patient. Don't utter my name again. Now Trenton I need another thirty six hundred seconds.

"Can't we just cuddle?"

"Now where's the fun in that?"

"Awe man be gentle."

"Again not fun."

"This pleasure is torture I don't know if I can withstand it."

"Let's get physical so you can retire your little pitcher."

"This is the real torture."

"You sure do have balls to talk, don't you?"

"And you have the lips to be disgusting."

"As you should know I don't mind an audience. But why does your ex and brother fornicating bother you?"

Lilith walks up to Lucian's cell barely clothed and proceeds to perform exotic dances while taunting him. She backs up against the cell. To his surprise the area she's touching disappears. She grinds on him.

"You miss this don't you? Remembering how I feel, aren't you? Oh look at you grabbing my hips huh? Well this isn't your's anymore." Lilith pulls away from Lucian. "That's funny you're jealous. How can you still love me after having a child with my sister?"

"She wasn't your blood sister and I loved you before you went insane."

"Insane?! Insane??! I'll show you insane." Without warning, Lilith opens Lucian's cell and with each word she speaks while walking him against the wall. Every word were like blades cutting him. "Is this insane Lucian? How do those lacerations feel? Hurts doesn't it? Those don't even compare to how you cut me. So sit there and bleed you some sense since you don't have any damn common sense. That was just a dominant tongue lashing. Maybe his words will be nicer. Don't bring me back in here."

"Lucian, are you alright?"

Coughing up blood, Lucian responds "I'm good. She just put a pain spell on me. I won't die, it just feels like it. But she messed up by bleeding me open."

"Really? How did she do that?"

"I can use blood magic to warn Lucy and explain our situation."

"Blood magic? Forgive me for always asking questions, but what the hell is blood magic?"

"You're forgiven because not most creatures know of blood magic. It's a dark power that can create manipulative objects and creatures. This magic is self aware and is like creating a life in the wrong hands the person using this magic would feel like a god. But let's start with that."

Lucian grabs his chest and collects blood particles from his open wounds. The blood forms into a ruby colored spider and crawls its way out of the cell. The spider scales the wall and finds a hole to escape through. Having made it out, the spider then turns into a red bird and flies off.

"So that spider made it out Lucian, how is it gonna help us?"

"It already knows what I need it to do because it's my blood with my memories and goals. It knows that it needs to find Lucy and protect her. Now we just wait and hope she takes to the wisdom I'm sending her way. So we wait."

As Jamal and Lucian let fate fly with the blood bird. Lucy is hard at work learning magical techniques with Re'nae unbeknownst to them both that they're truly mother and daughter. The blood bird flies at unbelievably high speeds. With the purpose of protection. The bird flies past the secret cavern before breaking through a voided vortex barrier. Reaching the other side to a sight of regal majestic buildings. A place with townsfolk,trade shops, and children playing. The bird flies straight to the biggest building that resembles a modern day mansion. It lands in front of the gate and forms into a version of Lucian with crimson frost tips in his hair and ruby colored eyes. Blood Lucian is greeted by guards immediately.

Without hesitation he says, "I'm here to have an audience with the queen. It's about her family."

After spewing those words, Queen Ophelia appears. "You have some nerve showing your face here Lucian. At least you could have graced us with your actual presence instead of a blood clone."

"Forgive me my queen. I would have come personally but unfortunately I'm imprisoned by your daughter."

"What??? My daughters are dead how dare you come here with more lies."

"Your majesty, I'm here because Lucy is in danger."

"Lucy... she's been found?"

"Yes, she was taken by Lily. Lily never stayed dead; she was resurrected by my brother shortly after she was killed. She now goes by Lilith but Lucy is safe for now."

"Where is she? Where is Lucy now?"

"She's with her mother."

"Impossible Re'nae is dead or is there something that was omitted from my knowledge?"

"I'm sorry my liege your daughter is alive and well I had placed her in a secret cavern just outside the barrier. The grave here is empty. I've enchanted her mind to forget our love and only hate me because she doesn't know Lucy is her daughter. In her mind Lucy is her niece."

"It's been twenty years since I last saw my daughters or granddaughter and now you're telling me they're all alive?"

"Yes but Lily has absorbed Liliths power and evil mentality. She plans to kill Lucy to hurt me and Re'nae."

"Well we mustn't waste time then because this little stunt you pulled is bound to have garnered her attention. My daughter is a lot of things. Controlling sure, overbearing certainly, but stupid isn't one of those things. We must bring my daughters home blood and grand and possibly adopted. You think you can save Lily?"

"I'm not sure but I will try."

"LUCIAN YOU STUPID ASSHOLE!!! You got word to mother and thought that was a good idea. Don't test my relationships. My mother is the most high of them."

"So your mama is your weakness?"

After saying those words Lucian was forcibly kicked in the mouth. "I told you to shut the hell up. Keep running your mouth and you will be begging for death. I might just leave you at the door and ding dong ditch that bitch. I don't care what we once shared anymore you try me again you're dead."

"She's hella pissed at you lulu."

"Yeah well I deserve her wrath. I played with her heart. I had a kid with another woman let alone it being her sister. I then killed her to save her sister from her. Through all that she still loved me until just then."

"Why just then? What happened in that moment?"'

"I saw blood and death in her eyes. She was willing to take me out."

"Yikes lulu and I thought she did you bad but damn."

"You know you get more lovably stupid by the hour Jamal. Tha hell is a lulu anyways?"

"Just a nickname."

"Don't call me that."

"Why not?"

"Because I don't like it."

"You don't like much do you?"

"Now you're getting it."

"Down the hall in the master quarters Lilith is irately talking to Trenton about the new circumstances."

"He went to my mother Trenton."

"It's lord Trenton."

Death glares at her twin flames brother explaining, "If I'm willing to kill the person I share the same soul with and have an intense, magnetic attraction and connection with just by bringing my mother into my business. What do you think I'm gonna do to his brother I'm only with because of sexual spite? Don't mistake me for a bitch who cares because I don't. Tread lightly before I murder you in his stead."

With visible fear Trenton realizes that he is out classed in power and malice. After the realization that he f**ked up Trenton frantically apologizes and offers his unadvised attention to Liliths rage filled emotions to quail her vengeful bloodlust.

"I'm sorry Trenton is fine so why don't we talk about what's bothering you."

"Your brother is a dickhead!"

"Ok let's start at the beginning."

"Beginning? Like how we met?"

"Yeah tell me."

"Well we met in the dark woods or dw for short."

"Why were you in the dw?"

"I was young and hot. I needed my fire to be put out. So I would take walks from the kingdom hoping to find a boy toy and on that day I found your brother. He looked helpless but he was just playing his role. As time went by we got closer to our first time sharing a kiss. We kissed on the tenth meeting and that same meeting we became entangled burning as one. It was amazing and liberating after that I went to my sister and pleaded for an audience with father. It was granted to my sister and I advocated for Lucian to be accepted into the kingdom. That was granted; he proved his loyalty to our family. All the while betraying me and leaving for my sister. Impregnating her and then trying to play house. So understandably I was pissed beyond the realms. A voice spoke to me in my head saying only three words, well really screaming them continuously, 'BITCH GOTTA DIE!' And i phucking Agreed. You sho right so I got Juliette's happy dagger to go show Romeo how love hurts. Later that night I was set to end her. I did kill her so after I slit her throat Lucian walked up on me. He told me thank you for saving me the trouble of riding your impotent sister so that our love can flourish once more. I smiled and dropped the dagger. We then embraced and shared a passionate kiss. After that kiss I was overwhelmed with infatuation and lust. I gazed into his eyes all giddy and giggling. He told me I love you Lily now and forever I put my finger on his lips and said I knew you loved me you silly ass. After we finished speaking Lucian ran me through with his blade. I looked to him and said you shriveled broke dick pig f**ker. He kissed me again and told me your mad know that I love you truly die with that knowledge and die with a smile. I couldn't help but smile. His kiss was magical even though the bastard ran me through. He continued to talk to me telling me this was an illusion but the hugging, kissing, and talking were real and that he did mean every word about loving me. But he couldn't allow me to kill my sister and their unborn child. I fell into unconsciousness riding the sweet release from the realm of the living. Until I was returned by you Trenton."

"Ok wow a lot to unpack there. So why is your mom so important?"

"I forgot to explain that because your brother gets on my nerves. But anyways Ophelia is everything I could ever ask for in a mother. She loved me for me. Accepting me, flaws and all. Even taught me magic that my dear sweet sister never bothered to learn. We were close and still are. So for Lucian to bring her into this that was the last straw."

"How are you with your father?"

"We don't speak about that bitch no."

"Ok, daddy issues a common trait in damaged hot girls. No wonder losers like Lucian get lucky with women out of their league. Cheating the system and manipulating the women. Why didn't I think of that?" Trenton mutters to himself.

"What did you say?"

"Huh?"

"If you can huh you can hear so out with it what did you say?"

"Oh I said it's a shame how men treat women in such a way."

"Uh huh miss me with bs Trenton I read your lips. You got one mo again to try my patience and that's yo ass. It will be prescribed and handed to you courtesy of foot in your dumb ass."

Gulping Trenton reluctantly says, "Yes, ma'am, it won't happen again."

"Do you know why me and your brother hurt each other but somehow better each other? It's because we thrive and grow off pain. It hardens us, pushes us and evolves us into something superior. The love is still there but what's love got to do with it after all power is what rules. Only fools fall in love and I'm a fool no longer."

Meanwhile in queen Ophelia's realm blood Lucian is leading the royal guard and the queen to retrieve the heirs to the throne.

"Alright we head through the dark woods first after we've passed through that there will be a special passageway. It was designed by me so only I can open it. A few words of caution. The dark woods isn't only just perpetual night fall it is also a living entity. This demonic place will feast on your dreams, fears, and sanity. With that said, no thinking impure thoughts. No thoughts of lust. No thoughts of beings or creatures after you. So for your safety think only safe passage. Because if you give into your thoughts the dark woods will destroy and devour you from within starting with psychological assimilation. After which if you're strong enough to fight you will become nourishment for the dark woods.

Do not attempt to save anyone but yourself otherwise their demise becomes your own. If you can't handle the task, stay here. To those who choose to venture further do so at your own peril."

Three of the twenty eight guardsmen withdrew from the mission. Stating their minds were battles from past wars on behalf of the kingdom and that their company would be detrimental to the mission. Knowing that these men can't leave one another behind if they should fall.

The queen respected their honesty and tasked them with protecting the kingdom upon her absence. "Watch over my husband as he sleeps."

The journey begins with all twenty seven travelers entering the dark woods.

"Remember to clear your mind. Safe traveles and clear passage.."

So far so good. Just then screams ring out and a guardsmen is swinging his sword wildly taking out three of his companions. Once realizing this Lucian positions himself whilst the assimilated guardsmen charges the queen. Without hesitation Lucian points two fingers toward him, locks his thumb down and pulls it up seconds later the doomed guardsmen is no more. Lucian shot him with a blood bullet putting him out of his misery. Now with twenty-three left, Lucian speak softly, mourn later, move now and think safe.

After another grueling fifteen minutes they find the secret exit and entrance to the cavern that housed Re'nae all these years.

"We've made it now once we enter through here, stay put until I explain myself to Re'nae."

"Blood Lucian opens the secret gateway all parties pass through safely."

"Now this place moves two days at a time your body will age half the time but your experience will double."

"Hey Lucian since you made that passageway can you create a new one that won't cause us to be in dire harm?"

"Aw, I'm glad you asked that question, smart one."

"Look at me, am I solid?"

"Yes."

"Am I solid now?"

"No. Alright I'm a blood clone my powers are limited to opening and closing gateways not creating. So thanks for trying to be cute and smart in one go but do us a favor and zip it dummy yeah. Yeah alright back to business I will get them up to speed then you come in my queen to solidify the truth."

As Lucian makes his way to the main chamber he leads the crew into a secret room where they can see what is transpiring at this moment.

With joy on her face Queen Ophelia is ecstatic that her girls are right in front of her.

"Now again stay here until I signal you."

"Re'nae you hear that?"

"What did you say, Lucy?"

"Hold on wait, that can't be."

"Hello Re'nae, long time no see."

"It is that sonofabitch how the hell did you find this place Lucian."

"I'm here for Lucy and you."

"I get why you hear for Lucy but why me?"

"I'm actually here to explain everything if you're willing to listen."

"I'm willing to kick your sorry ass in front of your daughter."

"Our daughter Re'nae."

"What did you say? The hell you mean our daughter?"

"Lucy is you and Lily's kid not me and you."

"That isn't true and I'll tell you why first off you're not dead."

"What?!?"

"Second I put an enchantment on you designed for you to hate me so you wouldn't come looking for me."

"OK he's got my attention Re'nae we should hear what he has to say."

"Thank you Lucy. Don't thank me yet after what Martin and Re'nae told me you got some explaining to do."

"What did they tell you?"

"Well, you got Re'nae killed. You betrayed my family and kingdom. Oh ,and my favorite, my mom's dead because of you."

"Well, that's all wrong because as I was saying earlier Re'nae is your mother. Also Re'nae isn't dead, she is under a hate enchantment designed for her to forget the true events of what happened and to hate solely me."

"But why would you put her in that state if what you claim is the truth?"

"Because your mother was about to kill herself after witnessing Lily's death. She saw Lily die and she saw me. I had killed Lily to save both you and Re'nae because Lily was possessed by a magic greater than mine. I was forced to put her down for your sakes."

"So Re'nae and you are my real parents?"

"Yes but there's more Lily has returned she was resurrected and upon her resurrection she revealed the truths she'd learned in death. Lily is the reincarnation of Lilith and she has inherited her powers. She has the real Lucian and your keeper locked away in her fortress along with your uncle that tried to overthrow the kingdom. She is now aligned herself with Trenton to eliminate you, Lucy. All for the sake of revenge against your mother and father."

"So she seeks to kill me because I was born? Like I asked to be brought here? I'm only here because I'm broken hearted looking for the one I love and then this happens like wow y'all really don't have anything better to do than to torture each other, screw each other, and kill each other."

"Well we live in a messed up society, what do you expect?"

"Ok I'm here too so why if this is true do I have an enchantment on me? I herd you mention that I tried to kill myself."

"Let me release you from the mental prison I put you in and all will be revealed."

Blood Lucian proceeds to unshackle Re'nae's mind, releasing her repressed memories. Revealing truths to the lies she has lived. As the enchantment is fading tears start to pour down Re'nae's face. Re'nae drops to her knees as the information processing in her mind begins to register as past truths and the information she just heard collides in her fragile fragmented mind.

"Lucian my love, how could you seal me away? How could you make me forget? Only to bring me back now."

"Lucy my beautiful daughter oh how I've missed you please come here. Please hug your mother for the first time."

"Lucian then interrupts and says, "I apologize my love. I thought it best to erase our love and your sister's demise by my hands from your memory but I have a surprise for you. It won't make up for the trauma I put you through but I will brighten your life."

"Come out my queen Lucian signals for queen Ophelia to make her presence known and without haste she appears."

"Re'nae is in shock seeing her mother coming out of a wall."

"Hello my daughters."

"Mom! Is that really you?"

"Yes my dear it's me oh how I've missed you. Lucy my granddaughter my how you've grown I could never forgive myself for losing you."

"Wait you're my grandmother and you lost me? How did this happen?"

"Oh I can answer that you see after Lily was killed Trenton used a forbidden resurrection ritual to bring her back. She snuck into your chamber after I enchanted your mother and brought her here. Your aunt forced out your spirit animal and you turned into a chocolate colored dove she then stole you and kept you as her pet. The keeper you seek was a little boy she took in because he had no family and your aunt is a sucker for strays because remember she was one. So now that you have a bond with your keeper and he has the same bond. Lilith plans to kill my real self, you, and the one you seek as a means to hurt your mother. Which brings us to the point of why we are here. Lilith knows about this place. We must return back to my kingdom, back home now."

After that exchange of words demons started rising from the ground.

"Awe, love the family reunion. Leaving so soon tho?"

Winged alligator minions appear in the sky behind Lucy and company stating, "Our master Lilith requires your heads. Kill everyone but leave the queen unharmed."

Queen Ophelia along with Lucian and Re'nae ready themselves for a fight aided by the remaining twenty one guardsmen. They attack the reunited family, taking out a few guardsmen and in return losing twice more demons.

"We won't win here, there's too many respawning as soon as we cut them down."

"Lucy you're my daughter you can make a gateway to your grandmother's realm once we get out of here."

With the remaining seventeen guardsmen nine stay behind to keep the demons busy and eight accompany the queen and her family to the barrier. Lucian tells Lucy to stick her hand out completely open and visualizes a wall with a hole in. As her father's words ring in her head she does as she told. She closes her eyes and sees the wall placing her outstretched hand on it. Pushing the wall she creates a small puncture closing her hand and sliding her fingers into it. She begins to stretch the hole open.

Meanwhile outside of Lucy's vision everyone is seeing the gate way opening before their eyes.

"Keep going Lucy. Lucy you're almost there."

Whilst Lucy is finishing the gate way the demons manage to overcome the guardsmen in the cavern and make their way to kill whoever is left.

Just before the demons make it out Lucy opens her eyes and says, "There, it's done."

"Lucian ushers everyone through with great haste every one makes it through. But Lucy goes last closing the gateway beheading the demon in charge."

Lucian asks, "Lucy, are you ok?"

"Yes I'm fine."

"Lucy opening realms can take a piece of you if you're not careful."

"Lucian the girls are home now I will train them to control their powers."

"Yes my queen but you don't know this magic."

"It's why you must stay and help train them as well."

"Are you sure my queen?"

"Am more than sure you have proven yourself noble not only saving me but our daughters from a terrible fate."

"Thankyou my queen shall we head home?"

"That sounds like a lovely idea I wanna catch up with my girls."

"After making it to the queen's home, Lucy asks, "Does this place have a name?"

"No I suppose it doesn't what would you name it?"

"I would call it Serenity castle."

"That sounds like Serendipity."

"Hey you asked I answered. Serenity is a fine name. Your father just used a big word to say that it's a good chance for some serenity here."

Like a maestro, Ophelia started moving her hands and reconstructing their home, renaming it "Serenity castle". It no longer resembled a mansion but once again was an elegant castle.

After constructing this new home queen Ophelia addressed her daughters. "You're my home, my peace, my love. No matter how much time passes by, you will remain that of which I speak. You are my passion, the force that breathes new life into the love you give me, you're my present and future. I love you all forever."

Without any indication of her presence, Lilith speaks from the severed demon head.

"Touching words mother surely you were referring to your blood."

"I didn't mince words you were included Lily. You should come home."

"Come home to what? My adoring sister stealing my man? My man having a child with my sister? My family writing me off like a dangerous debit?"

"Sister we were young we did foolish things I still love you come home."

"Loving someone who loves you but can't have you nor can you have them is torture in today society being faithful is being loyal to who you commit to but a punishment to your heart's true desires. Staying isn't straying but straying isn't necessarily the wrong direction. Love is blind it has no direction only a destination. Life is the ultimate test of faith and will. Free will is a powerful oppressor that isn't freedom but slavery. Sex is a slavery entertainment exhibit. A show for today's children to learn and perpetuate. This cycle only creates pain over pleasure. Crushing you from the inside out. Jealousy eats at you rage tears you apart depression slowly kills you happiness doesn't exist fear is solace death seems sweet. This is the human life it isn't perfect nor is it permanent. It evolves as we do as a people we thrive together and hurt alone. This is life and the trials that come with it some make it others unfortunately perish from the weight and struggles of their hearts. Joy, love, and pain are the teachers people are the lessons. Survive the perils these people bring or perish as a fool in love the choice is your's to make. And my choice is revenge I'll come home when all who betrayed me is dealt with. Heed me mother this is my final warning stay out of my way. Lilith you can come home please daughter say you'll reconsider.

"I will not end of discussion (click)."

"She hung up. How do you hang up a head?"

"Nevermind realized it as I said it. Lucian make a mess of that thing."

"Yes my queen Lucian then aims and fires completely eviscerating the demon's head from the inside out imploding every where. She sounded pissed and I get it she was done dirty by both of you."

"Lucy we can explain."

"Then explain it because it looks like she was utterly devastated by the ones she held close to her heart."

"Lucy calm down."

"No tell me why my aunt wants to hurt us? Why do you two love each other? Do you love Each other?"

"I love your father."

"Dad what say you?"

"I was sworn to love your mother."

"What does that mean?"

"Yes Lucy now come we must get you properly trained."

"Re'nae how long was i in the cavern with you?"

"Six days so three outside it."

"Where's Martin?"

"He was apart of the cavern he can't die so he's fine."

"Well damn he's lucky."

"Stop getting distracted we gotta focus on Lilith immediately."

"Your father's right. This doesn't feel right even still I must prepare for the worst."

Book
2

IMPOSTOR KING

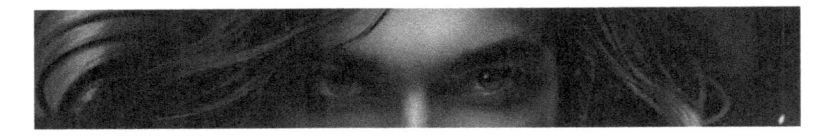

CHOCOLATE DOVE : IMPOSTOR KING

"My king our queen has tasked us to watch over you while she's away."

"Wait you aren't king Matthew! Who the hell are you?"

"Oh aren't I not your king?" the mysterious man says before shifting into king Matthew.

"Impostor," yelled the lead guardsman, charging with his blade drawn, cutting the fake king. "Where is our real king?"

"You ask the wrong questions often don't you?

"I grow tired of your insolence! Now what did you do with our king!?!"

"He's sleeping."

"Sleeping? Sleeping where?"

"That's not how this works I answered your question now answer mine."

"I'm not playing your games impostor."

"Don't you find it odd that I'm bleeding this much from a flesh wound?"

Realizing the impostors words caution sets in too late. Out of nowhere the two other guardsmen forcibly apprehend their new masters enemy. Kicking his knees out and forcing his arms behind his back.

"What are you doing Rodrick? Unhand me, O'Neal."

"Come now Logan, your fellow warriors are mine now."

"What have you done to them?"

"Nothing, they see you attacking their king."

"You're not our king!"

"In a few seconds you'll see differently."

"What are you talking about?"

"Remember my blood that you spilled out of me?" Taking his hand from his chest wound slapping Logan's face with his bloody hand. "You're my bitch now," he says as the impostor blood assimilates its self into his body and mind.

"How can this be?"

"Still with me, huh, Logan. Very well, I'll tell you. This a form of blood magic your mind will be mine in a few moments. For some reason, it's taking longer for your strong built ass. Ah, there we go. Now pledge allegiance to your king."

All in unison say, "Yes, my lord. We serve you. What are your orders?"

"Act normally and refer to me as your king. King Matthew! Forget anything of an impostor and do as your queen commanded of you. Watch over me as she has stated"

"There you are my king. What's going on in here?"

Before the Queen opened the door Matthew withdrew his blood back into his chest. "Nothing, just commending these three for their loyalty. You may leave. I must speak to my wife alone."

With that, the guardsmen take their leave.

"Oh do you now? Did I do something wrong my king?

"Not at all my queen I simply wish to speak with you.

"I don't know how to feel about that one.

"Just here me I love you my beautiful queen and I trust you blindly because of my faith in you being the love of my life that being said I know your faithful and I'm a jealous man a very jealous man I'm insecure about how a woman like you is interested in me it baffles me and encourages me at the same time it motivates me to be my best me for you the only downside is depression and feeling unworthy of you causing doubts about your faithfulness but I get over it because I know no man is me and I know no man can love you like me satisfy you like me or treat you like me because I'm your king and your my queen and no peon or servant can ever truly sit upon my throne and no slut or wench can ever truly approach yours so for our kingdom to flourish trust faith and love must be our conquering forces I love you deeply queen."

"What you tryna do get me hot and bothered?"

"Maybe. Did it work?"

"Come rescue your queen from this lustful situation she's been put in."

"Don't mind if I do."

The king and queen proceed to make hot and heavy passionate love behind closed doors. Some time has passed both king Matthew and queen Ophelia are cuddled up in bed together.

Matthew is playing with Ophelia's hair while singing:

"My lovely is oh so cuddly I love my lovely

She's so kind it baffles my mind

My lovely is honest and true without her I don't know what I would do

She's fair and also has gorgeous curly hair

My lovely is ravishingly beautiful also did I say meaningful

She's got mysterious sensual eyes when I gaze at them I think of heavenly sky's

My lovely is pure hearted about something's but I still know that she hasn't departed from me I'm so lucky

She's the love I never knew I wanted she is the love I don't wanna lose ever."

Ophelia is reacting to every word with different facial expressions. With them staring at each other, they begin to kiss again.

But in the midst of this, she stops Matthew, saying, "We mustn't continue, my king," while leaving the bed.

"Why the hell not my queen?"

"Our daughters have returned."

"How can that be? Aren't our daughters dead?"

"It was believed to be so my king. Some revelations were made."

"Revelations like?"

"Re'nae was never deceased."

"Our birth daughter was alive this entire time?"

"That isn't all Lily was returned from the dead and come to find out she's the reincarnation of my former enemy Lilith."

The impostor ponders this alarming information to himself. *Lilith will be detrimental to my plans I don't need an incursion to my plan this can not go unchecked.*

"Matthew, you with me?"

"Huh?"

"You were in thought about something."

"Uh, Lilith that information kinda had taken me back."

"Why? You think she remembers her encounters with you? If she does then she remembers me being her mother more."

"Why's that?"

"Because she warned me to stay out of the way of her and Re'nae's confrontation. To her I'm still her mother. Now get dressed your granddaughter wants to meet you.."

"Granddaughter?!? You mean Lucy is back here? So our family is whole once again?"

"For the most part yes."

"So where is Lucy now?"

"My guess is she's with Lucian, learning."

"Lucian's here?"

"Not entirely, a blood clone of himself."

"So, I've really missed a lot then?"

"It seems like you have so let's go catch up and put your pants on already."

"Alright, my queen."

We find Lucian and Lucy in the guardsmen training room where Lucian is explaining magical relics and powers that are available to Lucy through his power set.

"Lucy, do you have any idea what this is?" Holding up a beautiful necklace.

"That's jewelry dad."

"Don't dismiss this just yet. It is a necklace yes but the properties of the necklace is to house your clothes inside it. This is a charmed necklace that allows safe storage when I pass through the mirror in my animal kingdom realm."

"Animal kingdom realm?"

"It's one of your rooms in your mind. To understand you must first understand what you are."

"What am I father?"

"Well your a dark entity along the lines of demons and sorrow feeders. That's my blood heritage, but your also royalty of the light."

"Royalty of light is what exactly?"

"I don't know how to truly explain that but basically you can manipulate light. Your grandmother can explain more about her heritage and abilities later. Now it's time to learn about your rooms. Have a seat Lucy and clear your mind. Focus on the center points,align your breathing with your heart beat. Once you're in sync with your mind and body you'll access your mind's loft. This store your mirrors to your power realms. Each power realm has a room with a variant of your self. You must defeat each one to claim access to your powers."

Lucy focuses on meditation aligning her breathing with her heart beat. With a little difficulty at first but ultimately mastering the rhythm. Once Lucy mastered the connection to her center Lucian turned into a liquid state covering his daughter entering her mind. Lucy awakes in her self consciousness as she did before. Standing over her is a dove the size of her own body. Screaming in shock unaware that this is her spirit animal.

The dove speaks saying, "Calm down, Lucy. Goodness, you act like you weren't a dove before. You turn human for two weeks and forget that you were a bird for twenty years."

"I'm sorry but man you're huge no offense."

"My size is relative to yours. I am your animal variant."

"That you are so I was here before? Because I only remember being a bird for majority of my life."

"You came here as an infant. I took care of you when you woke up."

"When I woke up what do you mean by that?"

"You were in my form in the outside world but when you slept your consciousness came here back to your own body. Where I raised you until you left a couple of weeks ago."

"So you see what I see?"

"Yes once you open a room your variant inhibits the room. We kinda become your children in a way."

"So you're an extension of me."

"Yes now the necklace you seek is the closet next to you."

Lucy opens the closet and finds a whole wardrobe. "Are these my outfits?"

"Yes Lucy each time you pass through this realm you transform. So you do have outfits to choose from."

"So I'm you in the outside world right now?"

"Not right now we're both here."

"What does that mean?"

"When you pass through that mirror it will take you to the loft."

"The loft?"

"It's where the other mirrors are housed and where your father is now waiting for you."

"How do you know this?"

"I live in one of the realms of your mind when you open a realm we are connected to the rest of your mind conscious or unconscious. We become aware even if you aren't because your body and mind are our home."

"Alright I think I get it."

"Hey Lucy!"

"Yes!?"

"Put some clothes on!"

"Oh yeah sorry."

Lucy chooses a stunning pink tank top shirt with short sleeves and a black dragon skull on it. She then selects black jeans with lace sides. Then Lucy finds fingerless black gloves after putting her gear together she finds some versatile boots with breathable socks.

"Wow Lucy you look like you're ready to pummel faces."

"No I just like this style I need a hair tie so I can put my hair up."

"Look on the top shelf."

"Alright got it and I can't forget this. Lucy picks up a gorgeous silver necklace with a dove symbol as the centerpiece. Now my fit is set."

"Good luck Lucy now your father is waiting go continue your training."

Lucy proceeds to pass through the mirror seeing her father waiting patiently on her arrival.

"Well that's certainly a battle ready look there Lucy."

"Yeah the last look was kinda outdated. This one feels more tailored to me."

"Well looks good on you Lu."

"So dad about what I asked you. A few weeks back when I asked if you and mom loved each other. You said you were sworn to mom. What did you mean by that?"

"I promised your grandfather that I would protect your mother. In promising to protect her I also gave my life to her."

"But do you love her dad? Lucy love has nothing to do with this I swore my self to her. Before the king to give his daughter whatever she desired. To protect her even if it meant killing your aunt."

"Dad do you love mom or Lilith?"

"Lucy why do you persist with this question? Does the knowledge of my passion really matter to you this much?"

"It doesn't matter to me dad but it's more insightful to know how you feel. Knowing how you feel about mom and Lilith can make all the difference in your life. Letting mom know that you don't love her may hurt her but it will hurt her more to pretend that you do love her. When you still love Lilith."

"How do you know that!?"

"It's written all over your face the way you speak about her. It was on your face the first time I asked."

"Then why pester me Lucy?"

"Simple to understand my father and his decisions."

"Lucy this conversation is done do not mention a word of this to your mother."

"This is strictly between us dad. You will have to be the one who breaks moms heart."

"Why did you have to put it like that? This is why I had her enchanted to hate me forever. It was way easier to deal with."

"But it isn't right dad. You need to talk to mom and tell her the truth so she can let go of someone she never had in the first place."

"You're right Lucy I'll speak to your mother after your training and after we deal with Lilith."

"Thanks dad I just want you to free yourself and be able to confide in someone."

"Alright if we're done talking about this we got mirrors to explain. It looks like you have six with space for more. Which is weird I only know six from my blood line and I see all of them.

Animal,blood,enchantment,gateway,shadow, and time."

"Ok so you gonna explain those mirrors right?"

"Yes. So you know I have the ability to use five of the six. I can use all of these besides time. No one I know in my blood line can use the time realm."

"Ok well I'm from two blood lines but we'll come to that one when we face the other four. Because the spirit animal mirror is basically my stepmom."

"Alright well let me address the other four and what they hold starting with blood magic. Blood magic can be used to create blood clones like me. A blood clone will have red eyes and red tips or highlights in their hair. Blood clones don't share a connection to the creator until rejoining said creator. Blood magic can also be used for mind control,inhaling a mental space, or taking control of organs."

"Well that's twisted."

"Blood Magic can also create projectiles weapons. Next is enchantment this one is all about illusions both mental and physical. Pretty much straight forward. Gateway is the ability to create doorways to realms. It also can be used as a quick get away. Shadow is an ability that I haven't quite mastered but if done you will be able to teleport from shadows, puppeteer your enemies with their shadows and kill them by killing their shadow. Not only that but also create invisible weapons that cast shadows. To gain access to these abilities you must defeat or befriend your variants. A word of warning your variants are skilled and just as powerful as you are. You understand your tasks?"

"Yes father."

"Alright then select which ability you want to master and step through."

"Wait you aren't coming?"

"No this is all you. You'll do fine just don't die."

"Yeah no pressure dad thanks."

"So which one are you visiting first?"

"Shadow seems kinda inviting."

"We'll go for it Lu."

"Ok dad why are you calling me Lu?"

"I used to call you lulu as a child but now that you're all grown up. I think Lu is a good nickname."

"Ok dad I thought you were calling me that because Lily called you that or something."

"No sweetheart Lily called me Ian or lover."

"TMI dad!"

"You asked."

"Sorry I did but I guess Lu is a good nickname dad. Compared to the last few weeks I didn't even have a name so this a welcomed change."

"Lucy you're procrastinating."

"Am not I can go through anytime I want."

"Actually you can't there is a time limit once you select a mirror. Which is about six minutes. We've been conversing for about five and if you don't go through that mirror! you'll have to wait an hour which we don't have to waste."

"Ok ok I'm going, I'm going. I'm just a little afraid."

"We all are when it's coming of age season but you have to be strong and believe in yourself now go. Lucian gently shoves his daughter through the mirror to the shadow realm."

As Lucy passes through the mirror she finds herself surrounded by darkness. Falling through nothingness. Voices passing around her as she drops. Telling her that this where dreams die. Hope is snuffed out."

"You will fail the last thing she hears echoing in the back of her head."

Before hitting the ground wings expand from Lucy lowering her safely to the ground. Thinking to herself, wondering, *Did I just float with wings?*

"Yes."

"Who's there!?" startled, Lucy shouts in her mind.

"It's me luv your spirit animal."

"Oh you scared me I thought it was the shadow variant."

"No but you need to remember we're all connected. We need each other to survive."

"Why is this place black and white like I'm in a comic strip?"

"The shadow realm is just shadows. It's literally misery surrounding you. Pain,anguish, you name it, It's here."

"Sounds like depression and torture had a baby and baby went boom boom and made this place."

"Lucy just because this place is dark doesn't mean you have to be insensitive.

"This place is insensitive to my eyes."

While Lucy is have a conversation telepathically with her spirit animal, she is being watched by her shadow. The variant she's out to confront is right under her feet. As Lucy starts walking, she slowly realizes that instead of moving forward she is in fact going downward.

Hearing a voice but unable to see anyone. The voice speaks to Lucy. I told you that you would fail,"Now look at you, sinking in darkness."

"Lucy, focus on your back. Think about your wings," the dove says.

Lucy remembers how her wings feel and they extend just before her knees are taken into her shadow. She starts flapping her wings pulling herself up but not free. She flaps faster and faster so fast a spark flys out onto the shadow. Causing it pain and creating a chance of escape. Grasping the small chance she escapes her shadow.

"What the hell was that?" Shadow Lucy says rising up from the ground of shadows.

Floating in front of Lucy saying, "You wanna fly, let's fly." Charging Lucy but not able to hit her.

Surprised Lucy looks and asks, "What's wrong?"

Shadow Lucy falls back with an evil grin. Unbeknownst to Lucy the light is shifting behind her causing her shadow to get closer to shadow Lucy. Shadow Lucy begins to a baseball stance grabbing something resembling a handle.

Lucy is puzzled like, "The fu..."

Before she could finish speaking, Shadow Lucy swings the invisible melee weapon seemingly as though she never touched Lucy, knocking Lucy across the sky.

"Lucy, are you alright?"

"Yes, I'm fine, but my ribs are a little sore. What the hell did she hit me with? That Bitch Got An Asswhooping Coming!"

With Lucy about to charge her shadow, Dove stops her. "Lucy, stop!"

Lucy stops in her tracks, hearing Dove's words.

"Don't you see the shadows they're on her side she wants you to rush her. Look at her shadow she's holding something that looks like a bat or stick or something."

"So that's what she hit me with fucking bitch."

"Hey remember when you flapped our wings really fast and a spark came out?"

"Yes, why?"

"Try it a little more faster and see what happens."

"Alright dove let's see what we get."

Lucy beings to flap her wings while her shadow replica grin turns to confusion and anger. Lucy continues to flap her wings faster and faster so fast sparks begin to flare causing shadow Lucy to panic.

"What are you up to, failure?"

Lucy ignores her shadow and flaps harder and faster with her wings igniting. Fearing for her life shadow Lucy is petrified at the sight of Lucy's blazing wings. Lucy dashes forward beginning her attacks hitting her shadow with a barrage of blows. Knocking her to the ground and pushing her down.

With her shadow replica on the ground, Lucy says, "I don't wanna hurt you."

The shadow is surprised.

Lucy goes on to say, "You are apart of me. Stop this and join me be apart of my family," extending her hand out to accept the darkness of her mind.

Shadow Lucy takes Lucy's hand in defeat saying, "But I really wanted to win."

Lucy tells her, "You did, you have a family now."

She smiles at Lucy and darkness surrounds the two teleporting them to her room. Shadow Lucy reveals herself as an exact twin of Lucy with darker skin and a meeker voice.

PATRICK JACKSON

84

"Wow you look just like me."

"I am you."

"Do you have a name?"

"Yes it 's Lucy."

"Well I'm Lucy so I think nicknames are in order."

"Ok so what should mine be?"

"I was thinking you should have your own identity within my identity. So how's Susie?"

"I like it like Lucy but with my own twist."

"So Susie how do I use your power set?"

"To use my abilities simply feel your shadow that's me. When you connect with me visualize and attack as long as our shadow connects to the enemy whatever you conjure becomes your weapon in the shadows. It's an easy way to catch an opponent off guard."

"yeah I know you hit the hell out of me."

"Sorry like I said I was trying to win."

"So Susie how do I return to the loft?"

"Open the closet and go through the darkest corner of the room."

"Ok so go to the darkest corner of the room and."

"Oh welcome back Lu took you long enough."

"What you mean by that dad?"

"It took you nearly two hours to return."

"Damn I was just in there for all of twenty minutes. Time is decided differently in each realm you travel to. So be careful not to stay in one realm too long."

"Why not dad?"

"Because if you're not careful you can forget your own reality and become another resident to the realm you're in."

"Ok then how am I gonna know if I'm in too long?"

"Stick out your left hand."

"Ok!? What's this gonna do?"

"While Lucy wrist is out Lucian conjures a bracelet that has realm information embedded into it."

"Ooh cute af dad but what's it do?"

"It's gonna tell you everything you need to know about where you are give it a try."

"Ok where am I right now?"

The bracelet responds saying, "You are in the loft, the central point of your mind where all your variants converge. You currently have two variants in their rooms. Would you like to speak to them?"

"I can speak to my variants through a bracelet!?! Your lying!"

"Would you like to speak to a variant?"

"Yes which ones are available?"

"Animal realm or shadow realm at the present moment. Would you like speaker or telepathic connection?"

"Let me speak to animal realm on speaker."

"Right away Lucy connecting you now."

"Hello?"

"Yes. Dove is that you?"

"Yes but how are you contacting me because I hear background noises?"

"My dad created me a realm bracelet so I can communicate with my variants either by bracelet or telepathy."

"Nice Lucy so did you want something?"

"No not really was just checking on you and testing my bracelet. Also wanted to Thankyou for saving me back there."

"No problem Luv we are one without you I wouldn't be here."

"Thanks again dove I'll let you rest. Later Lucy."

"Thanks dad for this communicator."

"You're very welcome Lucy but we must go our time of training is over your grandparents are waiting to meet you after all these years."

SNAP!

"Huh what?"

Lucy awakes from her meditation in her new gear from the loft.

"Hello Lucy it's been a long time."

Lucy turns and sees a man resembling royal stature with long dark hair and a perfect black beard.

"I'm sorry who are you?"

"Why me? I'm your grandfather king Matthew."

"My grandfather? Really! Where grandma?"

"I'm right here Lucy."

Lucy is overwhelmed to have finally found her complete family. Lucian appears next to Lucy.

"Ah Lucian how nice of you to join us son."

"Lucian bends the knee and greets his majesties."

"So respectful this one come join us."

"Actually my king our granddaughter needs her training."

"Very well my dear we shall reconvene at dinner after her training is completed."

Lucy rushes up to her grandfather hugging him. Taken by surprise Matthew reluctantly embraces his granddaughter. During the embrace between the two Lucy feels jolts of rage in her blood causing her to jump back.

"Something wrong Lucy?"

"Nothing just a shock hehe."

"A shock huh?"

"Alright granddaughter off with you I need to speak with your father."

"Alright see you later dad, grandpa."

"You need to speak with me my king?"

"Yes but not here."

"So that was grandpa?"

"Yes Lucy what did you think of him?"

"Imposing, strong, beautifully crafted really."

"Well I see you took quite a liking to your grandfather."

"Hey let's not go that far grandma I still need to get to know him." Pondering to her self, *but first I need to figure out what that shock was.* "So grandma my dad mentioned that I'm a being of the royal light."

"Yes you are."

"I was wondering if you could enlighten me of our heritage?"

"Yes my child of course I can. There's nothing wrong with wanting to know where you came from. We are beings of light that inhabited a human being from the gontier bloodline. Our great ancestor was named Zephaniah Gontier. He sired your grandfathers great great grandfather Josiah Gontier."

"So my last name is Gontier?"

"Yes you're my daughters daughter."

"So Lucy Gontier?"

"Yes that's your name."

"Ok cool so why are we leaving serenity?"

"You think I'm gonna train you in my castle with the power we possess? Girl i don't have the energy to repair the damage we'll cause."

"You won't have the energy why not?"

"Because it's gonna be a draining process to properly train you. Under Ophelia's breath she mutters and Matthew put it on me a little too good."

"Come again grandma."

"No I'm fine. o what did you say?"

"Oh nothing worth repeating dear."

"Where are we going if we're not training at serenity. Serenity is supposed to be a peaceful place isn't it?"

"Yes but? I can't train you in a peaceful place. I can but I can't."

"That doesn't make any sense grandma?"

"I can teach you by explaining our powers and abilities or I can teach you by actually sparring. I choose the latter."

"Ok still doesn't tell me where we're going."

"Quit your belly aching we're here."

"We're where exactly? Looks like a bunch of nothing congregating with ain't shit here at a where the hell we going convention."

"Funny Lucy."

"Why thankyou I aim to please."

"Well you aren't short on Wit. So let's redirect that energy towards what we're doing. Alright now come to me Lucy."

"I'm here now what?"

"Grab hold to me?"

"What are you doing?"

"We're about to go inside."

"Inside where? There's nothing but mountains here."

"You are a magical being and still don't believe?"

"Hey I'm skeptical on a lot of things alright grandma."

"Fair enough Lucy. Walk with me carefully one misstep could have you falling off a cliff."

Ophelia and Lucy inch their way to the center position in front of the mountain side. Each step causes the wall of the mountain to shift and shimmer as if something is amiss.

"We're almost through Lucy."

Inching more and more towards the wall a light starts to shine.

"Lucy feel the light."

"What grandma?"

"Put your hand out and feel the light but keep hold of me."

Lucy put her hand out as does Ophelia. With both Lucy and her grandma reaching to feel the light they pass through a mirage barrier. Falling into the building Ophelia was leading them to.

"Welcome to the spar dome."

"Spar dome? Isn't that just a play on stardom."

"Stardom?"

"You know fame and high status."

"I already have high status Lucy why would I need stardom?"

"Why do you call this place spar dome?"

"Because we spar in this place and it's dome shaped."

"I guess you got me there."

"Not only that it's protected inside and out by our magic."

"So it's insulated?"

"Yes very much so. There are seats for spectators but that entrance is on the opposite side of the barrier. Located behind a small forest. It opens once you make through the forest. We came in through the competitors entrance. Ready to start our lesson?"

"Yes but could you finish explaining what we are?"

"We're light beings living in human vessels. I'll just show you but be careful we do need specialized garments. Here we go..."

As Ophelia focuses, her body tenses up. She begins to shine with her skin becoming light blinding Lucy. Ophelia dims her light down enough for Lucy to see her.

"You're completely light!?"

Ophelia turns her body back to normal but leaves her arms lit. "We control all forms of light. Electricity, fire, gamma and several other types including Fluorescent, High-intensity discharge, Infrared, Microwave, Rod cell, Ultraviolet, and X-ray. So if my science is correct we can create black holes, hear communication signals, cook things and see through people bodies. Oh let's not forget see people's body temperature imprints through walls. Your essentially a god Lucy particular over light."

"But light is used for so many things grandma."

"And all those things we have dominion over."

"So radiation we control that too?"

"Yes we can actually survive all of that in our light form. Our vessel form on the other hand well were susceptible to what kills humans."

"Ok so grandma I'm confused I thought you said grandpa was the holder of the light through his grandfather's lineage?"

"He is."

"Then how do you possess the light?"

"I'm glad you asked. The reason I possess access to the light is because I carried your mother and gave birth to her. The light is a giving light but it gives to the women from the sons of light. In simplistic terms have a baby with a man of light and he'll pass more than his offspring to you."

"So you got your powers by having mom?"

"Yes but it doesn't work in reverse. If you find a nice young man he'll be normal but your offspring will inherit your powers and abilities."

"Wow I so feel like I'm in seventh grade and I never been to school before in my life."

"Yeah that's another perk of the light super intelligence."

"Naturally born a smart ass now I've heard everything."

"You also have super endurance alongside super strength."

"Ok I'm hearing a lot of strengths but no weaknesses."

"Yeah those are emotional damage and blood loss. Emotional damage will block your abilities. Rage will increase them with a toll on your vessel. Blood loss is mainly for your vessel form but honestly anything that would kill a mortal will be fatal to our vessel forms. Let's get your light from going. Start by feeling the sparks in your blood."

"Sparks?"

"Yes that will help you ignite."

Lucy begins to search her vessel for the sparks inside her drawing out electricity and fire surrounding her area. Her skin slowly starting to glimmer with shines of glitter. Lucy gradually starts shining with sparkling gleams. Engulfed by the fire and electricity Lucy emerges into the sky as pure white light. With wings of light shimmering with sliver shine. Touching ground sparks of electricity and embers of fire crackles around her.

As Lucy inspects her new form Ophelia is stunned. "I have never seen this much power or wings like that."

"I guess I'm a different breed grandma."

Ophelia is immensely powerful but Lucy poses a greater potential.

"Wow Lucy you're gorgeous in that form."

"You trying to make me blush or something?"

"No I'm just impressed."

"So are we gonna get this party started or what?"

"Of course." Ophelia begins to take her form and the sparring begins.

Back at serenity king Matthew and Lucian secured a private place to converse.

"This seems private enough."

"What about the three guardsmen?"

"They're sworn to secrecy just as you."

"Very good my king. What is the issue you wish to discuss my lord?"

"Tell me about the night you killed Lily."

"I enchanted the room where Re'nae was housed. I was alerted and found Lily stabbing a pillow. I comforted her before and after I ran her through."

"You made sure she was dead? Yes my king. I cloaked her body after I watched the life leave her eyes. Then placed her in the furthest part of the dungeon. After leaving her there I went back to clean the blood that was spilt. I cleaned the blood then returned to retrieve her body but Trenton sprung his attack. In the mist of the confusion the cloak and Lily were gone."

"Do you know how she returned?"

"According to my creator Trenton resurrected her. She revealed that she was the reincarnation of Lilith."

"Your service is appreciated Lucian. O'Neal will show you out."

"Yes my lord."

"O'Neal come here!" Matthew whispers in his ear, "Henceforth watch for an opportunity to eliminate Lucian."

"Yes, master. Master, what do you want us to do about brother Trenton?"

"Nothing Logan. I need you and Rodrick here keeping the show going. Let Daddy handle Trenton."

Matthew starts hover, gliding backwards, and disappearing in the shadows. Transporting himself to a secret lair underneath Trenton's compound, he turns himself into his true form.

He walks to a sleep chamber, touches it, and says, "Hello, Matthew. Sleeping alright?"

After taunting his adversary, he creates a black fire and focuses on Trenton, watching Lilith give him orders.

Waiting for her to leave, he speaks, "Still the punk bitch, I see. I give you one thing to do and I return to see you whipped. Startled, embarrassed, and ashamed."

Trenton realizes his father's voice.

"Don't speak idiot, meet me in the underground lair now!"

Scared out of his mind, Trenton rushes down to see his father. Reaching him with an "I'm in trouble" nervous smile. He lays eyes on a man with a bald tapper fade resembling a muscular boxer with a clean shaven face. The man had a black suit made from shadows with said shadows swimming all over him the entire time.

"Father, what brings you here? You haven't been here for twenty years. Is there something wrong with Matthew's incubation chamber?"

"No, he's good, just change his fluids."

"Yes sir is that all?"

"No! Lilith, explain now!"

"Her... Well... when we created the confusion, I figured why not come from the dungeon. It's unguarded. You know, sneak attack, right? This girl sits up covered in blood incinerating my men screaming, 'Damn you, Lucian.' So Lucian killed the host and Lilith's spirit took over. What does that mean, Father?"

"OK, look, stop calling me 'father'. My name is Julius Draven. JD to you."

"Ok JD, so what's your take on Lilith?"

"The way I see it either the host died and Lilith assumed the body or Lily is still in there, a prisoner of her own body. Only time will tell. For now, stick to the plan and don't piss Mother off anymore than you already have."

JD turns back into Matthew, returning back to the king's private quarters.

In the spar dome flashes of light clash between Lucy and Ophelia.

Lucy asks, "I thought mom was supposed to be here?"

"Oh, I'm here."

An amethyst light shoots in between the silver and gold.

"Love the purple. By the way, why are you purple?"

"It's my signature color and you know we can fly without wings, right?" Why? Didn't Mom tell you?"

"No, she neglected to mention it."

"What can I say? I wanted you to feel special. But those wings are bad ass."

"Thanks, Mom. You think I could use them in combo streams?"

"Oh, most definitely. From what I can see, you're developing into a formidable fighter. You gave your grandma one hell of a fight. Now it's my turn."

"Mom, you're joking, right?"

Without warning, Re'nae charges her daughter.

Lucy braces herself. "Guess we're doing this, come on then!"

Lucy and Re'nae clash in a stalemate, blocking each other's strikes until they both connect. Lucy hitting her mother's face and Re'nae hitting her daughter's midsection. Knocking each other back with Ophelia looking on, watching her daughters blossoming into incredible fighters. Lucy retracts her wings and charges her mother, only to get close enough to expand and clash her wings. Creating a concussion blast, exposing her mother's shadow, and allowing her to pull her mother into a string of combos. Punches into a ballerina spin connecting with six wing slaps, ending with an ax kick. Knocking her mother out of the sky, Re'nae gets up.

Proud and pissed at her daughter, Re'nae pulls her arms back, yelling at her daughter, "Block this."

She throws her arms forward, connecting her index fingers and thumbs together, resembling a diamond. She screams, "Diamond smasher," firing a powerful purple blast, glittering as it rushes Lucy.

Perplexed at this, Lucy's wings wrap around her instinctively. Lucy is knocked out of the sky, hitting the ground wrapped in her wings, losing control of her light form. Re'nae and Ophelia rushing to Lucy with her wings retracting, revealing her battle-damaged vessel.

"Is she ok, Mom?"

"She'll be fine. We heal quickly."

Before they can move, Lucy she begins to stand up. But the light isn't in her eyes, nothing but darkness is visible.

The version of Lucy speaks to them asking, "Why would you attack your daughter like that?" Before engulfing her body in flames only to extinguish them revealing her wounds healed.

Awaking from the aftermath, Lucy asks, "What happened?"

"What did your daddy do?"

"Nothing but explain his heritage and help me access my central center.

"Central center?"

"It's where my powers are housed within my mind."

"That's too complicated but what I wanna know is what's with the fire?"

"Fire? I thought we wield fire and electricity?"

"We do, child, but you invoke it. Electricity and fire manifest from you when you transform. But what happened moments ago is concerning."

"Ok, so what happened?!"

"We'll tell you after we've spoken to your father. For now, let's return home."

"Alright, Grandma, but Mom, can you teach me diamond smasher?"

"Not today, maybe tomorrow."

"Fair enough. I am feeling famished after all that."

"Took the words out my mouth."

Meanwhile in Trenton's compound. Trenton is puzzled by the words of JD. *What did he mean when he said stop pissing mother off? She can't be the true be the true queen of the sorrowfeeders,* he thought to himself. *If this is true she is the mother of me, JD, and Lucian. But she was reborn with a human's body. So, ugh, forget it. She is my mother but not my mother. Stepmom?! Yeah let's go with that no blood relation, just spirit.*

"Where were you Trenton?"

"Checking the perimeter."

"Oh, did you find anything?"

"No ma'am, false alarm."

"Good, what news of the boy and Lucian?"

"The boy and Lucian are in good health and still confined to their cells. Ma'am, if I may ask?"

"You may."

"It's been a few weeks since the blood clone escaped here."

"What of it?"

"I was wondering what our next move is?"

"Don't worry yourself with such things. Counter measures have been in place since then."

"Yes, my queen."

"Lucian, it's been weeks. You sure your plan is gonna work?"

"Calm yourself, Jamal. Being impatient is sanity's enemy."

"You're saying I'll go insane if I don't relax?"

"Exactly so shut the hell up and continue to wait."

"Jackass I have questions so here bind yourself."

Lucian put on magical cuffs that binds his powers.

"Follow me."

"What are you playing at Lilith?"

"No playing Lucian just a simple interrogation."

Lucian follows Lilith to a room that is reminiscent to a dining room area.

"Have a seat Lucian."

Lucian takes his seat.

"You comfortable?"

"No not really. What the hell?!? Why did I say that?"

"Now that I know they work allow me to give you some full disclosure. I've spent the last few weeks crafting those bad boys for the little shit sitting in front of me. So this is how it's gonna go down. I ask you questions you answer truthfully because right now you're incapable of lying. You hungry?"

"Starving. Damn it!"

"We'll see if you eat. Why did you sleep with my sister?"

"Because I was sworn to her, as her betrothed."

"Who made you take this oath?"

"King Matthew."

"Why did you kill me?"

"I was was sworn to protect princess by any means necessary even if princess Lily attempted to harm her."

"By my fathers command?"

"Yes. Enough of this Lilith leave me my secrets."

"I wonder hmm. I need to know tell me did you ever love me?"

"I never stopped loving you."

"Oh! Oh damn uh?"

"You violated me and extracted the truth now you have no words? What did you expect me to say?"

"I wasn't expecting you."

"I expected you to tell me you love me too. To say that."

"Now you know the truth are we good here?"

"Yeah this is too much for me right now. Trenton!"

"Yes my queen. Feed your brother I need to process somethings."
Lilith leaves.

"What did you tell her that got her all bothered?"

"The truth."

"Well did you have to tell her?"

"Yes, she made cuffs that make me tell the truth now could you please stop asking questions?!"

"Did you tell mom I left a shit in the tub when I hadn't bathed yet?"

"Yes. That shit was hilarious."

"You asshole."

In the masters chamber Lilith meditates on the information collected from Lucian. Entering her mind she meets her reincarnation.

"He loves you."

"What are you talking about?"

"Lucian loves you Lily."

"He loves me and yet I'm a prisoner of my mind, because of what? Him killing me so please tell me how does he love me? I fashioned cuffs that renders the users Powers useless and doubles as a truthful tool."

"So you cuffed the truth out of him? I thought you had to be married for that to work?"

"Yeah no I just whipped up some old cuffs that were repurposed to bind his power and make him tell the truth. Cause I'm tired of his fucking lying ass."

"Ok well how do you know he loves me?"

"I asked him point blank did you ever love me? He replied, and I quote, 'I never stopped loving you.' But he killed me though. If not for you, I would be dead."

"He killed you because your father made him take an oath to protect your sister no matter what."

"But I thought he fell in love with her?"

"No he was sworn to her it wasn't a choice."

"So my father took the love of my life and made him leave me for my sister for why tho?"

"Look here I don't know why he did that but that's why we don't speak about that bitch here!"

"You gotta be a big bitch to do some shit like that."

"Who you telling? It's his fault you can't return to your body."

"But I'm alive because of you Lilith. Ok and I don't love your boy like that."

"If that were true why are you flustered?"

"I'm not I was just caught off guard. You know we share the same feelings Lilith. I can feel the sorrow beneath your rage knowing what you now know. Knowing the man that loved us continued to love us even while killing us. He secretly mourned us."

"The fact remains he killed us Lily."

"He stayed loyal to us Lilith search your memories think back to the dark woods. He promised us that he'll be loyal to our family."

"By killing us?! How is that loyalty?"

"Because we asked him to be loyal to our family for us. Not to be loyal to us. He did exactly what we told him."

"It's a little fucked up if you ask me Lily."

"Mixed signals can cause chaos Lilith."

"Wait chaos is that what father wanted?"

"I think we should pay his ass a visit."

"It's only right since he's been fucking up our life and orchestrating our death."

"I like the way you think Lily."

Blood Lucian returns to the guardsmen training room. Lucian feels an uneasy feeling before realizing that it's only O'Neal.

Oh it's you O'Neal have you come to train?

Yeah something of that nature.

Oh?!

O'Neal lunges at Lucian grabbing his throat attempting to squeeze the life from the blood clone. Ah trying to liquefy huh? Wondering why you can't? Alright since you gasped so nicely I'll tell you.

With Lucian on his knees fighting to stay conscious and not slip into deaths loving embrace. He hears O'Neal's words as he begins to explain.

"Lord Draven wants you dead. He gave me these here gloves that nullify blood magic which is why you're feeling cold. Your molecules are too cold to destabilize so you ain't going anywhere. Wow you're taking a long time die. It's starting to piss me off!

Lucian thinks to himself. *I need to do something or this information is going to die here with me.* Seeing O'Neal's shadow Lucian thinks. *This is gonna be a long shot but here it goes.*

Lucian begins to sink into the ground, smiling at O'Neal telling him, "Are you ready to go to hell with me?"

Lucian's eyes turn pitch black scaring O'Neal causing him to loosen his grip.

Now's my chance, Lucian sinks completely in the shadow.

"Where did you go insect?!"

"Oh I'm around but uh let's get somethings cleared up shall we?!"

"What are you talking about?"

"Who is Draven?"

"You dare speak ill of Lord Draven?! How dare you!"

"Ah shut up! Now look I have respect for you O'Neal so I won't kill you."

"Ha you kill me?!! Don't make me laugh. You couldn't even kill your girlfriend, let alone me."

Lucian materializes behind O'Neal, hitting him in the back of the neck. Rendering him unconscious.

"You were a father figure to both the king and I. There is no way you would turn on either one of us. You would give you life first so there is something egregious at play here. Forgive me, old friend."

Lucian opens a gateway to Re'nae's cavern shrine where he takes O'Neal.

"Lucian, what are you doing here?"

"Relax Martin, I brought him here because something isn't right.

Watch him while I enter his mind."

"Why are you intruding that man's mind?"

"I need to know what's after me and how to stop it. So watch him and all answers to your questions will be revealed."

"Alright Lucian, I'll do as you ask."

Lucian turns into a puddle of blood and begins entering his mentor's mind. Lucian searches O'Neal's memories, coming across the truth of who Draven is. A sorrowfeeder with advanced blood magic taking over Logan, O'Neal, and Rodrick. Seeing for his own eyes as Draven morphs into King Matthew and give the orders for his execution.

"I have to find O'Neal's inner self and free him from his imprisonment. But still what does Trenton have to do with this?"

"Wouldn't you like to know?!"

"Where's O'Neal?!"

"I'll do you one better, why is O'Neal?!"

"You test my patience. Where is my mentor?!"

"Kill me and you'll never see him again."

"I won't kill you but you'll wish I had!" Lucian stares at the mysterious creature until he yells, "Release"

"Release? That's it? How is release gonna defeat me? I don't know guy, looks like you win. Hey, were you going?"

"Oh bother."

"Wait, who said that?!"

"Could I trouble you for a jar of honey?"

"Get out of my head!"

"I'm scared of hefalumps."

"Shut the fuck up Pooh Bear."

"You're so rude, mister demon."

"I don't care. Stop existing."

"Stop resisting and give me a jar of honey."

"I don't have honey!"

"Sounds like you got this. I'll be on my way out."

"No! I mean stay a while. What's your hurry?"

"Well, Pooh Bear is in your head and I turned your brains to honey. So either you produce my mentor or die by a children's cartoon. Your choice."

"He's here in my stomach, unharmed. I'll give him to you after you free me."

"After? Do I look like a fool? Give me my mentor."

"Alright, alright, here."

"This really him?"

"Yes."

"No bullshit?!"

"None."

"O'Neal, can you hear me?"

"Lucian, is that you?"

"Yes."

"Where are we?"

"Inside your mind."

"You have your mentor, now free me!"

"Explosion!"

"Explosion?!"

"Do you hear him?"

"No."

"You're welcome."

"Nice doing business with you, I won't be coming again."

"Who said you could leave?"

"I wouldn't move if I were you."

"Screw you die!"

Lucian opens a gateway for the demon to run through transporting it above its previous position, exploding on re-entry. "Told him not to move."

"Lucian, please kill me!"

"I didn't come all this way just to kill you."

"Why do you care so much? Let me die, let me atone!"

"I've killed so many innocences for a fake. I couldn't kill an innocent man and you wouldn't be atoning if you killed yourself. So if you wanna atone, do it by living for the innocent people Draven had us kill."

"When did you get so wise?"

"I had a wise teacher and father figure."

"Thank you my boy."

"It wasn't a problem O'Neal happy to help.

"Promise me something Lucian."

"Sure what is it?"

"Promise me that you'll get that sombitch Draven."

"Done. Now I'll see you when you wake."

Lucian exits O'Neal's mind with him, waking immediately as Lucian materializes above him.

"Lucian, where are we? Who is that guy?"

"This is Martin, the keeper of this shrine."

"Shrine? What shrine?"

"This is Princess Re'nae's shrine in a secret cavern. Don't worry, you're safe here."

"Alright, I'm trusting you Lucian."

"That's all I ask. Now you settle in and I'm off to warn the others."

"Lucian, don't you want these gloves?"

"No, you keep them."

"But you defeated me when I had these. you sure you don't want them?"

"I'm sure and that wasn't you that I defeated. The true you has more skill and fight to wield any weapon you choose."

"You humble me, boy. Thank you for the kind words."

"No thanks are necessary. I spoke the truth."

"I appreciate that. I've held you up long enough. Go warn the others."

Lucian takes his leave as he opens a gateway to Serenity.

Meanwhile in the royal family room, Lucy hounds her mother.

"So Mom, can you tell me how to do diamond smasher?"

"I told you I would teach you tomorrow."

"Please Mom, just tell me how. Please!"

"No, Mom back me up here."

"I'm with Lucy on this one. I wanna know myself."

"Mama! Really?!"

"What?! What's the harm in explaining your technique?"

"Ugh, fine! You start by pulling your arms back with your fingers extended. Pull the power to your hands. When you have enough swing your hands forward fingers still extended. Connecting your index fingers and thumbs aim and fire."

"Sounds easy enough."

"What you mean it sounds easy enough?!"

"I said what I said. Mama, you know what?!"

"No, I don't know. How about you enlighten me."

The two woman throw punches at each other connecting the strikes but not to each other. Lucian appears in between the argument catching the punches with his face. Ophelia connects to the left cheek and Re'nae connects to the right jaw.

"Ouch!"

"Damn, they did Dad dirty."

"Oh hey Lucian, we were just looking for you."

"I'm so sorry, hun. that was meant for Mom."

"And if that would have connected, we would have been some fighting muthafuckers up in here."

"Why y'all so damn violent?!"

"Nature of The Beast Lucian."

"Well anyway, I'm glad you're all here. I have news to share."

"So do we."

"Ah, so this is where you all have been hiding."

"Grandpa!"

"Hello Lucy."

"Dad!"

"It's been years, Re'nae. I'm glad to see you."

Lucy and Re'nae rush Matthew to hug him.

"I see my queen has returned."

"Yes, my king, and you look happy."

"Oh I am, my girls are home. Oh Lucian, I didn't see you there. Why do you look so upset?"

"It's nothing the princess and queen decked me simultaneously."

"Now now ladies you haven't been home all of five minutes and already y'all are coming to blows?!"

"Mom started it."

"Don't you tell that lie!"

"Lucy what happened?"

"Hey my name is west and I ain't in that mess!"

Lucian takes the opportunity to sneak a message to queen Ophelia. On a piece of magical parchment. After giving her the parchment he motions her to read it in secret.

"Lucian may I speak with you a moment?"

"Yes my king. Read that to yourself."

Lucian and Matthew excuse themselves to converse in private.

"What's that Mom?"

"I don't know Lucian gave it to me and told me to read it to myself."

"Well go on, read it."

Ophelia reads the parchment as it states. *"Don't talk about anything training or strategy around king Matthew. It is imperative that we speak alone in the guardsmen training room bring Lucy and Re'nae.* Lucian wants us to not tell Matthew anything about our training."

"Why Mom?"

"That's what I wanna know myself."

"So we do as Dad says, right?!"

"Yes, if we want answers."

In the king's library, Lucian and Matthew converse once more.

"Lucian have you seen O'Neal?

"No, I haven't seen him since he escorted me out of your study, sir."

"Hmm strange, strange indeed."

"We should return to the girls before they kill each other."

"I hope not but you're right we should get them some food. You know how women are when they're hungry. I'm not trying to be Ophelia's next victim."

"Ladies, were back."

"Dinner anyone?!"

"Hell yeah Grandpa, what we having?!"

"Whatever your heart desires."

After the buffet style dinner, Lucian and the others try to escape the attention of Matthew.

"Matthew honey go on to bed and I'll meet you after I finish here."

"I'm gonna hold you to that Ophelia."

"Ok dear. Alright he's gone now come with me to the guardsmen's training room."

In the guardsmen's training room, Lucian begins to explain why they are there. But not before Ophelia make her thoughts known.

"What's this about Lucian? I hope you didn't make me miss an unnecessary dick appointment."

"You might as well cancel that."

Why say that Lucian?"

"Because King Matthew isn't King Matthew!"

"What the hell are you talking about?!"

"Dad, you're saying Grandpa isn't my real grandpa?!"

"Yes Lucy."

"How are you sure that Father is an impostor?!"

"King Matthew was replaced twenty years ago by a sorrowfeeder."

"No way, Lucian. Bite your tongue and stop your lies. My husband wasn't replaced."

"Ophelia, do you remember when you found Logan, O'Neal, and Rodrick in your royal chamber this morning with King Matthew?"

"How do you? How do you Know that?!"

"O'Neal was tasked with killing me after the first meeting with king Matthew. I traveled into his mind where I found a blood demon in possession of his subconsciousness. The impostor is named Draven he possesses advanced blood magic. This blood magic allows him to mind control and impersonate others."

"That explains the shock I felt when I first hugged him this afternoon."

"So you're telling me I've been sleeping with an impostor and a sorrow feeder no less?!"

"Unfortunately yes my queen."

"Ah hell naw! That bitch gotta die!"

"I almost forgot why were you guys looking for me?"

Without warning Lucy starts to produce steam from her soft skin. Her eyes turn pitch black. Fire begins to escape her body and surround her.

A dark voice come from Lucy saying, "Mother has arrived."

"Yeah, you see that?!"

"Uh huh."

"That's why we were looking for you."

"I've never seen that before."

"Mother is here!"

"Where is she going?!"

"I don't know Ophelia but we have to help her."

CHOCOLATE DOVE

Lucy, engulfed in flames, leads her parents to Lilith in the grand hall.

"Mother." Lucy kneels to Lilith.

"Oh, a child of hellfire here?! Interesting how one of my children managed to get here."

"Lilith, what are you doing here?"

"Hello Mother, I'm here to kill Father."

"Not before I do myself!"

"Huh ok what is going on here?"

"Come with us and we can explain and strategize a response."

"Lucian's blood clone is here huh? So what is this strategy meeting about?"

"The king you seek to kill is a fake."

"Interesting but why does that concern me?"

"My brother Trenton has something to do with this."

"I know you hate betrayals but we're on the same side here."

"Enough Lucian she won't listen to you."

"Mom what are you doing?"

"Quiet girl this is between me and your sister."

"What's this?! Mother you approach me with what purpose?"

Ophelia walks up to her daughter slapping her then embracing her. "It takes some backwards bullshit to bring you home. I've missed you and your sister. I love all my family and you're no different."

"Mother?!"

"Yes, my dear, I mean this with all my heart, come with us. We can't stay here. Lucian, open a gateway."

Lucian opens a gateway to the secret shrine with everyone, including Lilith, going through. After Lilith's epiphany and change of heart, the Gontier family works together exchanging information.

"Lucian, is it done?"

"No, O'Neal. Change of plans."

"I see you brought the royal family."

"Yes, they weren't safe there."

"Uh anyone care to tell me why the psychopathic sister is with y'all."

"She's with us Martin."

"Yeah two weeks ago her flying gator demons were here eating his fellow soldiers. So you sure about that?!"

"We loose men in wars, even dumb ones. But if they were protecting the queen and princesses, then they died with honor."

"Who is the child of hellfire?"

"Child of hellfire?"

"What's that Lilith?"

"A child of hellfire is a child of yours and mine. A direct descendant of my power."

"So you're saying my daughter is your daughter as well?"

"Oh, so that's Lucy in there?! What power she holds. What untapped power!"

"Can you bring her back Lilith?"

"Why? She's beautiful in this form."

"Lilith, bring my granddaughter back now!"

"Alright. Damn, you guys still ain't no fun. Died and came back and that stick is still up y'all ass." Lilith snaps her fingers, releasing Lucy from the fiery form.

Lucy falls to her knees, unconscious from the fire that consumed her.

"What was that Lilith? What? That form what is it?"

"That form is simply rage and desperation igniting."

"Why is it happening to Lucy without her knowledge?"

"I don't know, Lucian, maybe she's slipping into it. She's been training and unlocking her powers, right?"

"Yes."

"Ok, then she needs to master all of them before she can control the hellfire."

"What can we do for now, Lilith?"

"Nothing really. Just keep her calm and hydrated."

"Now, what's this about Trenton having something to do with this?"

"The sorrowfeeder named Draven. Who impersonated your father for the last twenty years."

"Twenty years?! So Draven made you take that oath, not Matthew?!"

"How do you know that?"

"I forced it out of you, well, the real you."

"How did you go about doing that?"

"Truth cuffs."

"What are truth cuffs?"

'Handcuffs magically designed to make the wearer speak only truth when asked questions."

"Well, aren't you intuitive, Mother?! A real student of the game, aren't you Mom?!"

"Lilith, calm down. It's common sense and I used it to torture criminals back in the day."

"Grandma, you were that bitch back in the day!"

"What are you talking about? I'm still that bitch right now."

"Ok, on to more important things like Trenton's involvement in this."

"We can go ask him."

"How do you suppose we do that, Lucy?"

"Lilith, you can transport us there with you, can't you?"

"You think I can get all of us to where Trenton is? If there was two of me maybe, but not by myself."

"What if I use hellfire?"

"I thought you were unconscious when I was explaining that!"

"No, I was conscious, just not in control."

"So your flames took over your body. I think I have an idea. Think of someone you truly hate and focus the hate into your hands. Then give me your hands. Everyone who's going, grab hold to me or Lucy."

Lucian and Re'nae grab ahold of Lucy while Ophelia grabs on to Lilith. Fire surrounds the five consuming them, transporting them to

Trenton's compound. Lilith lays out the details for a plan of action.

"Lucian, Lucy, and Re'nae you three go to the cells and release Jamal and Lucian."

"Who's Jamal, Lilith?"

"He's the boy that grew up with you and took care of you."

"My keeper?!"

"Correct Lucy. Now when you get to the cells you will need to tap into hellfire magic. You won't need the flames, just my essence. Once you tap in just want the cell doors open and they'll open. Lastly DO NOT touch the bars! The bars are enchanted to turn prisoners into part of the cell."

"Well, that's all kinds of messed up."

"Re'nae, life is messed up look at what we're doing now."

"Point taken, but still isn't that a little extreme?"

"No, it's discipline and incentive to do right instead of being spoiled shits."

"Ok Lilith, you have your reasons and we're past that now, so back to the plan."

"Mother and i will find Trenton then meet back with y'all in the interrogation area.

Where is that exactly?

Lucian will show you now go we don't have time to waste.

Which way?

Straight behind you.

After giving out directions Lilith and Ophelia begin to look for Trenton. Lucy and her parents look for Trenton's prisoners.

So Lilith will you come back home?

Depends on how this goes.

What does that mean?

It means if all this manipulation betrayals stop then I'll consider it.

I just miss my daughter.

You think I don't remember our battles Ophelia?!

If you remember that I know you remember how I raised you!

You raised Lily who's now dead.

Doesn't mean you're not my daughter.

We were bitter enemies, why do you want me to comeback to a place that was never my home?

You lived in Lily, Lily lived in serenity until she died. Serenity is your home! As for the enemy aspect all I see is my gorgeous daughter.

No not gorgeous now. You really want me to come back home that bad?!

Mothers and daughters fight but the love is real remember that.

Why do y'all gotta play with heartstrings?!

What do you mean Lilith?

Between you and Lucian I'm conflicted. The more I learn about how and why I died. The more I feel certain about coming home but. Before that happens I must finish this story. I have to know why my life was relegated to being insignificant.

Let's find out together, don't do this alone.

Thanks mother for the unyielding support.

You're my daughter and apart of my family you will always have my support.

It's not much further now.

How do you know?

I can sense his thoughts and track him.

What is this room?

Trenton what are you doing?

Nothing my queen!

Come with me and bring those cuffs.

Yes my queen do we have a new prisoner?

Yes and no.

Before Trenton could understand what Lilith's words meant she cuffed him.

My queen why am I cuffed?!

You're gonna answer questions about Draven in the interrogation room.

Oh no please no!

Why not?

He'll kill me!

Shit! Let's go meet up with the others.

On the other side of the compound Lucian and his family reunite in the holding cells area.

I can see the souls trapped in the bars. Mangled corpses mashed together.

What are you talking about Lucy?!

She can see the enchanted dead.

Lucian oh how I've missed you!

What are you doing here I told you to keep them safe!

Things have changed I'll show you once we're whole again.

Lucy eyes begin to steam she holds her hands centered. Pulling them apart from each other while saying open. The cell doors burst open. Re'nae and Lucian embrace each other with Re'nae kissing him passionately. Lucian stops Re'nae and collects his blood. Blood Lucian rejoins his creators body syncing the blood clones memories and power advancements.

Lucy take Jamal and leave us the room.

Why dad?

I made you a promise it's time to make good on it.

Now tho dad?!

Knowing what I know now is the only time that is appropriate now leave!

Lucy leaves slightly upset with her father.

What was that about Lucian?

Lucy made me promise to tell you the truth.

The truth?!

I don't want to hurt you so I'll just say it. I don't love you.

CHOCOLATE DOVE

Visibly heartbroken, Re'nae continues to listen.

I took a secret oath to be yours and protect you from harm. Going as far as killing my beloved under false pretenses. I hope you can forgive me for letting you fall in love with a lie.

With tears in her eyes Re'nae rubs her hand on Lucian's face and tells him. That bitch gotta die slow for being a hoe ass piece of shit.

You, your sister, and your mama why they gotta be bitches? Why they gotta die?!

You gotta be a big bitch to play with my life now I gotta end theirs.

I get that Re'nae but why so violent?!

It's in the blood.

So are we good tho?

Yes Lucian I can't make you love me. I don't even know why I fell for you the way I did. I know Lily was head over heels for you. I guess I wanted to make my father proud. Enough of this feeling sorry shit we got to get back to mom.

Yeah the interrogation room I know where it is.

Let's go then.

You guys alright?

Yes Lucy were all good.

Ok well Jamal is still unconscious so?

I'll carry him follow me. Lucian leads his family to the interrogation room where Lilith and Ophelia are.

Hey guys did we miss much?

No Lucian we haven't even started.

Yeah how's it feel to be free?

I don't know let me try it.

Huh?!

I love you Lily!

Blushing Lilith is shocked still wondering if what Lucian said was real.

You look puzzled I said I love you Lily.

Lilith turning red hides her face and continues to start the interrogation.

Lilith starts questioning Trenton. Who is Draven?

He's my father. I'm dead! I'm so dead!

Is he my father as well?

Yes.

What is Draven planning?

To impersonate Matthew Gontier and rule the realms.

Why did Draven make Lucian take an oath of protection?

To feed off his misery.

Why did I have to die?

You are Lucian's true love. What better way to feed off his misery, than to have him kill his beloved.

Why did Draven have Lucian swear his life to me?

To combine the light and sorrowfeeders' power through an offspring that can be manipulated to be his weapon for controlling the realms."

So Draven is my grandfather?

Yes child he is your grandfather and you are his master plan.

Is my husband alive?!

Matthew is alive.

Where is he?!

In the room that you found me in.

Take us to him.

As Trenton leads everyone to Matthew, Lucy asks, "Why are you doing this with Draven? You seem nice."

"Matthew was the cause of my mother's death. This was to avenge her, but thank you for the kind words."

"I don't believe that Matthew killed your mother."

"Grandma he's wearing truth cuff it doesn't get much truthful than that.

I mean I'm sorry for your loss but I know my husband."

"Your husband was literally replaced for twenty years, so do you?! Do you really?!"

"Oh, I don't like him."

"Grandma he's right we don't know what grandpa is really like."

Stunned at the thought of Matthew being a murder Ophelia remains silent.

We're here.

Where is he?!

The incubation chamber at the end of the room.

Ophelia dashes to the chamber, eager to see her true husband. "Open this thing now! Release my husband."

Trenton opens the chamber, knowing his father will arrive moments after the chamber's unsealing. "You all have mere moments before Draven arrives."

"That's fine, we want his ass anyway!"

"Don't underestimate him, Draven is formidable," Matthew says while getting his witsabout him. "Trenton, I heard the fallacies your father told you."

"I want no part in your lies, you killed my mum. The only person to ever love me!"

"That's just it. I didn't kill your mother because I was already in the chamber by then."

"What are you saying?! No, that can't be right! I saw my father's defeat after you killed my mother."

"That was an illusion masterfully crafted by Draven."

"Enough! Enough of your lies!"

"I knew your mother Trenton. I knew her well because she was one of my royal consorts in secret before I married Ophelia."

"How dare you speak of my mother in such an outlandish way!"

Matthew begins to sing, "Sleep, my child, and peace attend the all through the night. Guardian angels God will send thee all through the night. Soft the drowsy hours are creeping, hill and vale in slumber sleeping, I my loving vigil keeping, all through the night..."

How do you know that song?!

I taught it to Scarlett when you were a baby.

What?!

I named you Trenton because you're my son.

That can't be true! You're not my father! I don't have the light so you're lying!

You don't have the light because you were born with angelman syndrome.

You're wasting your breath, Matthew. That idiot just doesn't understand. He's weak just like his mother and even you couldn't save her."

"You bastard! You killed my mother!"

"Trenton, wait, the cuffs!"

Before Trenton could realize this, Draven puts out his hand and shoots a blood ball in Trenton's face.

"Now I've Killed You Closing His Hand Imploading His Head, Killing Him Instantly.

Trenton's lifeless body falls like useless debris as Draven turns his attention to the rest of Matthew's family.

"You guys get out of here I'll kill this piece of shit. Lilith, was it? What's this about you killing me? I gave you simple instructions to kill your sister but what do you do?! You get your self killed by my son, no less. I should be thanking you because his misery was already tasty. Your death was a delicious cherry on top. His anguished soul was oh so intoxicating but you had to ruin it."

"No one asked you to come back! That voice in my head that was compelling me to kill my sister that was you?!"

"Guilty!"

"Why would you do this to us, especially your own son?!"

"Girly I would do this to my own mother. I guess I already did tho. I mean Lilith's here Lily's dead so hi mom! If it wasn't clear I'll do anything to be all powerful! You lot aren't anything to me. By the way Matthew, Ophelia is top notch. Best hoe I've hit in my life! Hahaha!"

Lilith started feeling intense rage, telling Draven, "I've vowed revenge against my family, tried to kill them. All because of the realm's dumbest bastard! You've pissed me all the way off!"

Flames start to pour out of her eye sockets, finger tips, and mouth, creating a fireball above her head so incredible that Draven starts to seconded guess himself. The flames of the fireball begin to cascade and swirl around Lilith. as the flames dance around Lilith's body. She begins to sing the song Matthew sang moments earlier. Filled with anger, pain, and sorrow she sings, "Sleep, my child, and peace attend thee all through the night. Guardian angels, God will send thee. All through the night. Soft the drowsy hours are creeping, hill and vale in slumber sleeping, I, my loving vigil keeping, all through the night."

Realizing this transformation every one is stunned. Draven is annoyed and forced to endure the transformation.

"While the moon her watch is keeping all through the night. While the weary world is sleeping all through the night. Over thy spirit gently stealing, visions of delight revealing, breathes a pure and holy feeling, all through the night."

Lilith's hair become horns. Her wings expand, resembling death angel wings. Her top burns off, turning the ash and soot into her clothes.

Burning, steaming, Lilith continues, "Deep the silence round us spreading, all through the night. Dark the path that we are treading, all through the night. Still the coming day discerning, by the hope within us burning, to the dawn our footsteps turning, all through the night."

Draven is visibly uneasy about Lilith's presence, causing chills in his blood. "It's so hot, why am I cold?!"

"Star of Faith the dark adorning, all through the night. Leads us fearless toward the morning, all through the night. Though our hearts be wrapped in sorrow, from the home of dawn we borrow, promise of a glad tomorrow, all through the night."

Finishing the lullaby, Lilith's queen of demons' form is revealed with glimmers and glimpses of hellfire bursting off her skin. Rage is personified across her body she speaks softly to the remains of Trenton.

"Rest my child, be at piece with your mother for you have served me well."

"Don't tell me you actually care about that... that waste of sperm."

"Draven, you managed to do something only your son has achieved."

"Oh what's that?!"

"Piss me off to an asswhooping state."

"I'd like to see you try!"

"Remember, I'm your mother. I just sung you a lullaby. Now I'm gonna finish the story by whooping your bitch ass. Then I'm sending you to time out in hell! Get out of here, Mom, Dad, and you four go. Leave him to me."

As Ophelia and her family clear out of the underground lab, Draven attempts to attack Lilith's family.

"Where do you think you're going?!"

Lilith cuts Draven off before reaching anyone, allowing them safe passage out. "I told you that you were getting your ass whooped! This is between me and you. Now face your mother like a man, you baby bitch bastard you!"

"Why, you disrespectful old whore, how dare you talk to your superior like that!"

"Superior?! More like delusional I created your ancestors' ancestors. What power could you possibly have superior to mine own?!"

"Shut up, shut up, shut your mouth!" Enraged, Draven clashes with Lilith, proclaiming her death by his hands. Punching Lilith's face, Draven cuts his knuckles open. Enjoying the damage he's inflicting as each blow opens his wounds more and more.

Unimpressed, Lilith asks, "Are you done? I hope that wasn't your best because if it was, you don't stand a chance in heaven, hell, or purgatory. That ass is about to be tenderized and seasoned to perfection after mama's done! You are nothing! Weak with false sense of power. You don't understand that you've pissed off the wrong woman. Not even that, the wrong creature. You've pissed off the ultimate bitch. I kill for amusement. You kill for necessity to ensure your feeble plan comes to fruition. We are not the same. What did you accomplish besides sleeping with Ophelia for twenty years? What power have you garnered? Face it, you're a pathetic excuse for a deformed embryo that should have died in the womb." "I will not stand for this fulmination!"

"Seems I've hit a nerve."

Tired of Lilith's antics, Draven prepares to end this fight. Draven pounds his knuckles together, crystallizing the blood. As he pulls his fists apart, blood blades take form.

"So you wanna use blades?! Well then, let's start cutting! Lilith grabs her horns ripping them off. Squeezing them in her hands as they grow and sharpen. Lilith's horns regrow back after creating her own blades.

"Come at me, chicken shit!"

"Your foul words do nothing but infuriate me. So do me a favor, when I kill you, stay dead!"

"No dice, ass clown! I won't die until I have your soul in my hands, strangling it like a stress toy."

 "Good luck with that, bitch!"

"You call me that like it's a bad thing."

As they cross swords, the mutual hate is shared. Draven is emasculated further by Lilith's words. Her words ring true to his core, enraging him. He salivates at his lust for her demise. Draven sneakily liquified the tips of his blades.

Lilith clashes with him again but this time, blood splashes in her eyes. "Ah, you sneaky bastard you!"

Draven takes the opening, stabbing Lilith's heart and slitting her throat. "Now you die and stay dead!"

As Lilith falls, dying, she hits the ground inches from Trenton's body. Draven relishes the sight of death by his hands. After admiring his devilish work, he turns his attention to the rest of the vermin that he needs to exterminate. Given the headstart Lilith gave them, Lucian had time to plan a course of attack. In the midst of this, Jamal wakes from his weakened state.

"You finally with us?! Had enough beauty sleep?!"

"Don't mind dad are you alright?"

"Yes but who are you?!"

"That's Lucy my daughter. You were the bait to get her here remember?!"

"Yes I do but why are we out here?"

"Because Lilith found out what we all found out. We were played all of us!"

"Played by who?!"

"Draven!"

"Who is Draven?"

"A despicable sack of shit!"

Oh, wait who are you?!"

"I'm Lucy."

"Grandmother, please save the pleasantries for a time when we're not in peril. If Lilith can't defeat Draven on her own. Then we attack him together. Jamal and Matthew, stay hidden; this is gonna have to work with the four of us. You three transform and dim yourself to blend in. I'll serve as the distraction."

In the distance, Draven can be herd yelling his accomplishments and destroying the compound.

"Where are you royal cunts!"

"Draven, out here!"

"Who has the balls to call me! Oh, if isn't my arrogant son! Tell me, how was killing O'Neal?! Did you cry after you ended him?!"

"Actually, he's alive and well; free from your control. I knew about you before I returned."

"You weak bastard! I've killed your mother, brother, and lover! Now I will end the disappointment that is you."

While Draven is boasting, Lilith's blood beings to boil. Boiling Until a Fire Ignites Lighting The Blood Trail. Burning Like a Fuse To Dynamite.

With that eruption a hellish scream was released with it yelling, "DRAVEN!"

"No, it can't be!"

While Draven was distracted, Lucian took his shot signaling his family's attack. Yelling in unison, "EXPLOSIVE BLOOD BULLET! THUNDER ARROW!" And a mother-daughter combination, "DIAMOND SMASHER!"

While this is going on Lilith was revived with the hellfire inside of her. Realizing she's back in the living realm. She picks up Trenton's body transporting him and her to the shrine. A scared Martin and intrigued O'Neal witness Lilith in her QOD form.

She tells them watch over his body. "I will bury him when I return," leaving as quickly as she came.

Returning back to the battle, all four attacks connected. Obliterating Draven into fragments. Everyone powered down and regrouped.

Jamal was surprised, exclaiming, "I can't believe that worked!"

Lilith appears through fire beside Jamal, scaring him shitless.

"Aye yo it's trying to kill me! Lilith you're alive!"

"Yes, where's Draven?!"

"We just obliterated him but he said he killed you."

"He did but I can still sense his smug ass!"

After declaring she could still sense Draven, a shadow portal formed behind Lilith. Seeing this, without hesitation, Re'nae grabbed her sister, hugging her and spinning her to safety, but positioning her to see her sister impaled by a blood spike. Lucy watches in horror. Lilith is stunned by her sister's selflessness.

"No, no, no, no, I didn't want this anymore. Stay with me sister!"

"It's alright Lily, you deserve happiness. Just promise me that you'll protect our daughter."

With those final words, Re'nae dies in Lilith's arms. Crying holding her sister close, Lilith shows her humanity and the pain and sorrow are overwhelming.

"Ah damn that shit tastes good!"

"You! You soulless, heartless, FUCKER!"

"Wow Lucy, didn't know you had it in you."

Underestimating the seriousness in Lucy's voice Draven dismisses Lucy until silver light fills her eyes. Huge black wings shoot out of her back. The outline of the wings are blinding silver with electricity sparking. The inner wings are pitch black with flames bursting and burning. Her hair is normal, but streaking with flames. Somewhat like highlights but with fire. The electricity and flames in her wings combine. Electricity sparks from her skin.

"You killed my mother, so hear me and hear me well. I will kill you. I will erase you. I will be your END!"

Draven Is Taken Aback And Shocked About How Much Power This Girl Has. "What is this?!! What is that form?! I've never seen such a thing!"

Lucy charges Draven in a blink of an eye. By this time, he is airborne. Lucy is relentless in beating Draven. She breaks his face in, breaking his nose and arm. Bitch slapping him from left to right, completely dominating him until Draven starts feeding off Matthew, Lilith, and Ophelia's pain because of Re'nae's death. He starts to rally and take over the fight.

"Lilith, Lilith can you hear me?!"

"Re'nae, how are you communicating with me?!"

"My vessel is dead, but you can absorb me into yours. You would have access to my power."

"Would I be myself?"

"Yes, you would be in control."

With that, Lilith and Re'nae combined each other's power. Lilith turned into a beautiful angelic demon creature with the same look as Lucy but amethyst eyes and outline of her wings.

"What not you too?!"

"Get your fucking hands off my daughter, you sorry BITCH!"

Lilith-Re'nae shoots upwards to join her daughter's fight. She connects to her family's minds telepathically, telling them that Lilith and Re'nae are combined as one being. She pleads with her family to let go of the sorrows because she isn't dead.

Then she spoke only to Lucy. "Let's hit him with a double diamond smasher!"

"That won't work."

"What if we use hellfire and call it diamond smasher flame?!"

"That could work, Mom, but we have to keep him still. I got it! Mom, get behind him and make his shadow appear."

"What good will that do?"

"Trust me."

"Alright Lucy, now what?!"

Lucy connects her shadow to Draven's, holding him in place. Draven knows he's screwed if he doesn't do something now. He begins to telepathically communicate with Logan and Rodrick. *"I need you two to shadow port me out of this! I'm between two opponents and can't move! I know they're going to try to desecrate me with extreme malice."*

While Draven is calling his minions, Lilith-Re'nae and Lucy are charging.

"You ready to fire this thing, Mom?! Let's burn this bastard bitch!" Lilith-Re'nae fire in unison, "DIAMOND SMASHER FLAME!"

The attack was mesmerizing from Lucy's side, sparkling silver with glittery electricity wrapped in fire. From Lilith-Re'nae's side deadly dark amethyst with terrifying electric force swarmed with fire. Unable to move, Draven is forced to endure intense pain and punishment, maiming his flesh and disfiguring the once handsome devil. The attack lasted forty-five seconds. Draven only endured fifteen seconds before Logan and Rodrick showed up opening shadow portals, redirecting the demonically gorgeous attack upwards. Creating an opening for retreat, Logan and Rodrick carry their mangled master through a portal.

Seeing this, Lilith-Re'nae charges them, but the portal closes before she reaches them.

"Damn, they got away!"

"They'll be back. That egotistical piece of shit will want his pound of flesh."

"Come on, let's go lay his victims to rest. Lucian, open us a gateway out of here."

"Yes, my king."

Lucian takes his family to Re'nae's shrine where they catch up. Before anything takes place, Lilith enters her mind. Finding that Lily and Re'nae have reconciled their relationship, becoming sisters once more.

"Re'nae, thank you."

"For what?"

"Your selfless act reconnected me to my humanity. You helped me find my heart."

"You're my sister even if you declare that you aren't, Lilith. I didn't see any difference between you and Lily. So the fact remains I would give my life if it meant saving my sister. I'm glad I got to save you."

"I don't know what to say."

"Go live life for us, Lilith. Re'nae already told you."

"Told me what Lily?"

"You deserve happiness, now go protect my niece. Train our

daughter well."

"Lilith, you alright?"

"Go, they're calling you."

"Hey Lilith?!"

"Thank you truly."

"We'll be here."

"Lilith?! You alright?!"

"Yeah, sure Lucy."

"You sure because I was calling you for a good minute."

"I'm fine."

"Ok, well come on, Grandma and Grandpa are waiting. They want to give Mom and Trenton a eulogy."

"Good, everyone's here. Let's get started. Tonight we are laying both my son and daughter to rest. My son was misguided, used, and betrayed. His life was stolen from him just like his mother before him. My only regret is that I didn't reveal the fact that he was my son earlier in his life. May he find peace with his mother. To my darling daughter, giving your life to save another is beyond bravery. You showed true honor and heroism. Losing you just when I return is the worst feeling I could ever feel. I can only imagine how your mother feels to finally have you home safe and alive. To only bring you back two weeks later dead again, this time for real."

"Aw Daddy, that's so sweet. But you don't have to be sad."

"What?! Re'nae, is that you coming from Lilith?!"

Yes! I tried to tell you guys earlier. Allow me to explain. (in Lily's voice) I'm Lily. I'm also (in Re'nae's voice) Re'nae. My full name as it stands now is Lilith Re'nae Gontier but you can call me Lily. I know you all prefer that anyway."

"So you're my daughters and my wife's most powerful enemy?!"

"Yes, Dad and Mom, you get your daughters back, they just brought a friend along".

"That's fine by me. Come here, my daughter."

Ophelia and Lily embrace as she welcomes her home.

"Ok but what about Re'nae's body?!"

"Dad, that's my vessel; it died. All my memories and essence is in Lilith. All three of us are one."

"I'm so conflicted."

"Don't be, Matthew. It's alright. Let's get these two put to rest."

"There's already a casket here for my vessel. Lucian left it here. We just need one for Trenton. What is he? About five-six, five-seven? I'll make him one five-eight just to be safe."

Lilith transported a nice mahogany casket for Trenton's body. Lucian lifts his brother's corpse and places him in the casket. while Lilith lifts Re'naes and places her in her casket. The two are buried side by side. Ophelia redesigns the monument plaque to read: "Here lie the royal children of Matthew and Ophelia. They are gone but not forgotten. The memories they have made will keep them alive in our hearts. They will be missed for the time being but we will be together again. A family once more."

After the dead were laid to rest, Lucian recounts what happened with Draven to O'Neal.

"So y'all didn't kill the fuck?! Well, I guess I can settle for his ass getting burned on both sides like a piece of fried shit!"

"Yes, but he still has ahold of Logan and Rodrick."

"Don't blame yourself, son. You'll save them. For now, enjoy your family. I see you eyeing her, go talk to her."

"So since my mom and my aunt are in you, does that make you my auntiemama?!"

"Sure Lucy, I'll be your auntiemama. But I'm your mother in public."

"Is everyone ready to go home to Serenity?"

"I'm ready, me boy! Been ready since you set me free from that demon."

"Lucian, go ahead and take us home."

Lucian opens a gateway to the grand hall with his family and father figure.

"So what are y'all gonna do now?"

"I'm about to hit the mess hall. See ya."

"Well, I'm gonna get a cup of coffee and reconnect with my wife after these twenty years. In other words, do not disturb!"

"Come on Matthew, I need all of that!"

"I think we'll go too. We need to get to know each other. I feel like we can finally get closer than a boy and a bird could ever get now that I'm in my human form and not in a cage. I don't think I'm ready!"

"Come on Jamal!"

"So um... Um, do you wanna... Do you wanna go catch up?"

"YES! PLEASE TAKE ME OUT OF THIS FUCKING AWKWARD SHIT RIGHT NOW! Take me into my room and TAKE ME!"

"Well, yes ma'am!"

While the Gontier family reconciled and reconnected with their respective lovers, a threat still lingers in Draven.

Recovering in a dark desolate undisclosed location, he lies, seething at the fact that his beautiful body was tarnished and declaring to himself that he will have his revenge.

"I will destroy Matthew and his little family. I will decimate my own flesh and blood. He's dead to me. I will be the ruler of this world and all the rest! My granddaughter will help me or watch more of her loved ones perish. This is not where we end. No, this is just the beginning. I will have my power restored and my enemies broken, battered, and beaten beneath my feet, begging for the sweet release of death!"

Printed in the USA
CPSIA information can be obtained
at www.ICGtesting.com
LVHW010621011224

797923LV00015B/645